T0064738

NO FORWARDING ADDRESS

PADDY STEWART

Order this book online at www.trafford.com
or email orders@trafford.com

Most Trafford titles are also available at major online book retailers.

© Copyright 2013 Paddy Stewart.
All rights reserved. No part of this publication may be reproduced, stored in a retrieval
system, or transmitted, in any form or by any means, electronic, mechanical, photocopying,
recording, or otherwise, without the written prior permission of the author.

Printed in the United States of America.

ISBN: 978-1-4669-7677-1 (sc)
ISBN: 978-1-4669-7676-4 (e)

Trafford rev. 02/062013

Trafford
PUBLISHING® www.trafford.com

North America & international
toll-free: 1 888 232 4444 (USA & Canada)
phone: 250 383 6864 ♦ fax: 812 355 4082

CHAPTER ONE

Reynaldo fidgeted nervously in the front seat of the sheriff's car. The long ride had been exhausting and he felt a little nauseated. Although his probation officer had told him some things about the drug treatment facility, he was unprepared for the tall, chain link fences that surrounded an assortment of red brick buildings. The setting sun beyond the pine trees cast long, somber shadows.

Two wide gates screeched an ominous welcome as they slid open, allowing the deputy's car to enter. They were greeted by a uniformed security guard, who seemed neither friendly nor threatening. The guard took Reynaldo's small duffle bag which contained all his personal possessions, and ushered him into a small room equipped with a vinyl covered examination table. Reynaldo's dark eyes darted about the room, like a trapped animal. He wondered what was about to happen.

A tall, gray-haired man, wearing a white jacket and a stern expression, appeared. He carried a clipboard.

"Reynaldo, I'm Dr. Benson. We need you to remove all your clothing, so we can search your body for concealed drugs. I'm sorry to invade your privacy, but this is necessary. Just try to relax," he said, while pulling a latex glove on one hand. Being surrounded by three men who were much bigger than himself, he felt completely helpless, and knew he had no choice in the matter.

The deputy left the room, but the security guard remained, going through the contents of the duffle bag. He inspected every item of clothing while Dr. Benson inspected Reynaldo's body cavities. The coolness of the air-conditioned room and the trauma of the humiliating experience caused Reynaldo's teeth to chatter. He desperately wished he had a few "white crosses" to make him feel better.

After the two men left the room, with instructions to "get dressed", an unattractive, unfriendly nurse approached while he was still bare to the waist. She carried a syringe and a rubber tourniquet.

"Hold out your arm," she demanded.

He obeyed, knowing he must follow all instructions in this institution if he wanted to get out any time soon. The deputy reappeared, standing near the door. Reynaldo was uncertain whether he stayed to protect the nurse from him, or him from the nurse.

The nurse's name was pinned to her stiff, white uniform. Nancy Pitchford, R.N. Reynaldo flinched as she sunk the needle into his vein, piercing his dark, tough skin. He was almost certain she meant to hurt him. Most junkies would not be the least bit bothered by a needle, but Reynaldo had never "shot up". He had only smoked joints, popped pills, and sniffed inhalants since the age of nine.

As she untied the tourniquet, Reynaldo watched with frightened black eyes as the syringe filled with his own, dark red blood. The nausea he had almost forgotten washed over him again. She handed him a clear, plastic cup.

"Urinate in this. Over there." She nodded toward a closed door.

Reynaldo shut the door behind him, uncertain whether he could obey her order. But, he was afraid not to obey the scary nurse, so he turned the faucet on for a few seconds and complied. He also took advantage of the opportunity to throw up. Then, he felt a little better.

"Dr. Benson will see you again in the morning," she said, throwing his shirt at him. "Put this back on. Mr. Hanson can take you to the detox wing." She turned toward the stocky deputy. "You remember where it is, don't you? Down the hall, to the right, then turn left."

Reynaldo fumbled with the three buttons still remaining on his faded, blue striped shirt, and then reached for the small duffle bag.

"Leave that here," Ms. Pitchford commanded. "Security may not be finished with it."

He followed Deputy Hanson down a short hallway and turned left down another hallway which led to an open door. There, they were met by a male attendant wearing a green "surgical scrub" shirt over a pair of Levis. His name tag said . . . Larry McBride, LVN. McBride and the deputy shook hands. Obviously, the two had met before. Probably, Mr. Hanson had transported others here.

"Welcome to 'The Pines'." This guy, McBride, seemed friendly and harmless.

"He's all yours," Hanson commented, turning to retreat down the hallway. He took a couple of steps and turned again. "Oh, Rey," he said, pointing a finger. "I hope I don't see you again." Reynaldo managed a facsimile of a smile. He knew what the deputy meant.

He had been arrested countless times for numerous offenses . . . truancy, theft, shoplifting, public intoxication, and criminal mischief. Following his last arrest, after being involved in an aggravated robbery with Rudy and his gang of "Los Banderos", his probation officer had made arrangements to send him to this facility for adolescent drug abusers. Some of the older boys were on their way to prison.

"If you get with the program, you can be out in six months," Jim had told him. "Then we'll decide what to do with you." Jim Hagerty was his fourth probation officer since his first arrest, five years ago. Reynaldo wanted to do right, but he just kept messing up.

"Over here, Rey," the attendant beckoned. "You can have this bed." He pressed his fingers against the mattress of a hospital type bed. "They tell me these beds are uncomfortable, but it won't be long 'til you'll be moved to a regular dormitory. Everything is nicer over there . . . including the nurses."

McBride's statement seemed to confirm Reynaldo's opinion of Nurse Nancy Pitchford. He did a quick survey of the room which contained four identical beds, all lined up against one wall. A row of small windows on the opposite wall were covered with venetian blinds. Several chairs and four night stands completed the furnishings. The bed at the far end of the room was occupied. The person lying there had long, black hair and appeared to be asleep. Reynaldo couldn't tell whether the figure was male or female.

"Several of the patients are in the day room, watching TV. It's another hour until lights out," McBride said, looking at his watch. "Come on. I'll show you where."

They walked through an office area that was separated from the patients' sleeping area by large plate glass windows. Beyond the office, another room with beds was visible. "That's where the girls sleep," he said.

The person with the long black hair must be a guy, then, Reynaldo decided.

Two boys and a girl were in the spacious day room, listlessly staring at a television screen. They were each smoking a cigarette. One white boy lay on an orange vinyl sofa on his stomach, his chin resting on folded arms. He had a very bad case of acne.

"This is Rey," McBride announced, as he ushered Reynaldo to a chair with cigarette burns disfiguring the gold vinyl covering. The boy on the sofa grunted and an expression, resembling a sneer appeared on his face. The tall, black boy stood and shook Reynaldo's hand, limply. "Hi, Rey, my name is Charles." He displayed a toothy grin. "Did you just come in?"

Still feeling weak, Reynaldo nodded. They all looked at him with knowing expressions; each of them having endured the same humiliating procedures. The girl, with stringy blonde hair and too much make-up, giggled.

"That's Francine . . . and that's Murphy," the black boy said, introducing the other two.

In limited conversation with Charles and scattered comments from the others, during commercials, Reynaldo learned a few things about his immediate surroundings. The three patients in the day room had been in the detox unit for a week, under close supervision for withdrawal from drugs. With steady progress, they would be dismissed to a regular dormitory soon. Reynaldo had no drugs in his system when he arrived, although it felt like he had a hangover when he and the deputy started out early that morning.

McBride told him there were two other patients currently in the detox unit . . . the boy he saw sleeping and a girl, who was being kept in seclusion. The girl, after three months of treatment, was allowed a pass to go visit her family. She came back high on cocaine. Now, apparently, she was back to square one.

After the lights were out in the sleeping area, Reynaldo lay on his back on the hard mattress, staring at the patterns on the ceiling. A dim light remained on in the office area, where McBride sat waiting for a relief worker who would come in at 11 P.M. A female nurse came in periodically to check on the dude with the long black hair, who had begun to moan and flail around in the bed next to Reynaldo. Charles and Murphy were snoring rhythmically in the other beds.

Reynaldo was frightened of this new place. He had been held overnight in jails several times, but he knew he would be released the next day to his Aunt Maria or to a probation officer. Now, the only people in the world who might care about him were many miles away.

McBride had been replaced by another attendant when Reynaldo finally fell asleep. He dreamed restlessly. He was back at the wheel of the get away car as Rudy and two other guys were robbing the liquor store at gunpoint. An alarm sounded, and red and blue lights flashed. Something began to choke him, and he gasped for breath.

Suddenly, Reynaldo's eyes popped open as a figure hovered over him. Strong fingers were clenched around his throat. Reynaldo grabbed the assailant's arms, but could make no sound. After minutes, that seemed like an eternity, the overhead lights flashed on and two attendants came running.

He still couldn't see his attacker's face. It was covered with long, black hair.

CHAPTER TWO

The attendants, one male and one female, grabbed the assailant's arms and twisted them behind his back before propelling him out of the room. By that time, both Murphy and Charles were awake with puzzled, sleepy expressions.

Reynaldo was coughing and rubbing his neck when the female attendant returned. It was Nurse Nancy.

"Are you all right?" she asked coldly, as if it didn't matter whether he was or wasn't'. Reynaldo tried to speak but no words would come out, so he just nodded.

"He just had a bad reaction to his medication. He'll stay in seclusion for a while." She switched off the lights. "All of you go back to sleep."

But, Reynaldo couldn't. He remembered the time when he'd taken a bad spill off a bicycle-a stolen one—when he was about ten. His arm and face had been scraped badly on the gravel road and hurt real bad. He desperately wanted someone to hold him close and make him feel better. He felt like that now.

Reynaldo's mother died when he was barely two years old, and his father, an alcoholic, had just disappeared. No one knew where he was. Aunt Maria had tried to take care of Reynaldo, but she had four children of her own. She and her husband, Reuben, moved around a lot, looking for jobs. Since he was thirteen, Reynaldo had mostly stayed with friends, older boys who were consistently in trouble. Just before his last arrest, Jim Hagerty had placed him in a foster home and got him started back in school. He was fifteen and only in the seventh grade. This arrangement lasted barely a week before he got mixed up in the robbery while he and his friends were all high from huffing ether.

They had done it at a friend's house, a girl whose father was a doctor. The process was simple. They just sat around a table with a pan of hot water in the center. Then, they covered their heads with a sheet while someone put a few drops of ether in the water. The substance was easily available to the girl, and it was just one of many things the kids used to get "high".

Although the venetian blinds were closed, Reynaldo could see the first light of morning. He wondered what his first full day at the institution would hold.

Soon, he was sitting in front of Dr. Benson, feeling very small and insignificant. He was also uncomfortable and embarrassed because of his previous encounter with the doctor. Dr. Benson set down his cup of coffee and picked up his clipboard. He half-sat on a corner of the desk nearest Reynaldo's chair. His manner and expression were kind and gentle, a stark contrast to the foreboding Nurse Nancy Pitchford.

"You're a little bit anemic, Reynaldo, which is not unusual for the kids we get in here. We'll give you some vitamins and we insist that you eat three good meals a day. You seem to have a kidney infection, so we'll need to check on that periodically. Tomorrow, we'll get some X-rays and have a dentist look at your teeth. Right now, we need to give you a shot of penicillin for that infection. He stood up. Reynaldo squirmed, thinking about the needle.

Dr. Benson ushered him to the same room where he'd first encountered Nurse Nancy. It was still early morning, and Reynaldo was afraid she would still be there. Sure enough, she came in carrying a hypodermic needle.

"Drop your pants," she demanded. Reynaldo hesitated. He wanted to ask her to put it in his arm, but he was speechless before this intimidating woman. So, he reluctantly complied, and felt the burning sting in his hip.

Before he had zipped his pants, a tirade of screaming, emerged from somewhere down the hallway; the nurse turned abruptly to go investigate.

Later, in the day room, the others were discussing the patient who was just admitted that morning.

"She was coming down off a bad trip man," Charles said. "I know how that is, man. I've been there. It makes you crazy as hell."

Reynaldo had never taken acid. He just liked the high he could get from booze, popping pills, or huffing.

"What will happen to her?" Reynaldo asked the black boy.

"Oh, they'll just keep her in seclusion until the stuff wears off. She'll be all right in a few days." He gave the impression that he was an expert on the subject.

Reynaldo summarized that there were now three patients in seclusion; the girl that came back high from her pass, the dude that tried to choke him, and now, this new chick on the "bad trip". He wasn't sure what seclusion was like, but he hoped he wouldn't find out.

Two days later, at breakfast, the dude they called Chino appeared, carrying a tray of food. He sat down opposite Reynaldo, who watched him warily. Apparently not hungry, he pushed a helping of scrambled eggs around his plate, and fixed his slightly dilated eyes on Reynaldo. Finally, he said, "I'm sorry, man. I was hallucinating. I didn't mean to hurt you." His English had no accent. He smiled slightly, revealing a chipped front tooth.

"Hey man, it's cool. Don't sweat it." Reynaldo replied, sizing up this guy with the long black hair. "What drugs you been doin?"

"Just marijuana; some primo. You ever done primo?"

"Sure," Reynaldo lied. "How long you been here."

"A week. Man, you'll probably be out of this fucking place before I am. That's the second time I've freaked out since I got here."

Reynaldo was distracted by the appearance of a girl he hadn't seen before. She was very petite, with a smooth, olive complexion. Her dark hair was long and straight. Reynaldo thought she was beautiful.

"Her name is Carmelita Crain," Chino said. "I knew her in Dallas. We were in the same crowd for a while."

Reynaldo was somewhat embarrassed by his obvious interest in the girl. There had been a number of girls in the gangs he ran around with, but he'd never had a real girlfriend; at least no one that he really cared about.

"She got busted for hitting the stuff on her weekend pass. She's already been here three months. Now, she may be here six more."

Reynaldo's eyes connected with hers for a brief moment, before he quickly looked away.

"You like the looks of that chick, little buddy? "Huh?" Chino looked amused. "Well, maybe I can fix you up with her somehow." The amusement left his eyes, revealing a kind of cold, calculating shrewdness. "We'll just have to see about that."

That night, Reynaldo again watched the patterns on the ceiling, still remembering Carmelita's face. He wondered what Chino had meant.

The next day, he was moved from detox to a regular dormitory. He wondered when he would see Carmelita again.

CHAPTER THREE

Reynaldo and Charles were escorted by an attendant to their new quarters, a one story brick structure somewhat larger than the one they just left. Reynaldo carried his small duffle bag, getting a first real look at the place that would be his home for the next six months. At least, he knew where he would be for that long-but then what?

This is not so bad, he thought. Even the fence and locked gates didn't seem to matter. He didn't have any place to go anyway. A man on a riding lawn mower passed in front of them. The grounds were lush green and several varieties of colorful flowers grew around the trees.

They were met inside the dormitory by an attendant called Rusty. He was a big, muscular guy, who looked like he could take anything or anybody in stride. He showed them to their beds.

"You'll be staffed this morning," Rusty said, as he showed them where to put their things. "That means you'll be assigned to a caseworker, and they'll decide what groups and classes to put you in."

"Classes? Here? You mean we have to go to school?" Reynaldo asked with a look of dismay clouding his face.

"Sure, punk," Charles teased him. "That's part of our problem, don't you know? We're dumb. We don't have no education."

A reluctant smile appeared at the corner of Rey's mouth. Charles was always joking and clowning—the good humor man. He stood a head and shoulder taller than Rey, and his grin seemed to fill his face, displaying a set of big teeth. His skin was the shade of a Snicker bar and a bushel of kinky hair crowned his head.

Reynaldo liked Charles, but he hated school. He always did. He still remembered his very first day of school, when, at the age of seven, he started three months behind all the other kids because his Aunt Maria and her family were moving around so much. He started out behind the others his age and never caught up.

The introduction to his caseworker came later that morning. Rusty escorted him and Charles to a large, two story building with many offices. Reynaldo was nervous. He instinctively knew he would be spending a lot of time with his caseworker and wondered what kind of guy he would be.

Reynaldo was left standing in a small, cluttered office with many posters and plaques on the walls. The name plate on the door said—Juan Rivera, Social Services. Reynaldo learned, later that most of the Hispanic patients were referred to Rivera's office.

A rather handsome man with a thin mustache and sideburns looked up from a stack of papers and smiled. "Hey, man, how you doing? Did you get settled in the dorm?" He stood and reached across the desk to shake hands. "Sit down." In contrast to Nurse Nancy's demands, Rivera's directive was more like a polite request.

Reynaldo sunk down into one of the two chairs placed near the desk. Rivera uncovered a folder and looked at it briefly. "You're from San Antonio?"

"That's the last place I lived."

"Your probation officer thinks we can help you here. Do you want to be helped, Reynaldo?" He looked up, with an eyebrow raised above his steady gaze.

Reynaldo was not sure what he meant, but he nodded his agreement.

"I see you've been using a variety of drugs, and getting in a lot of trouble. We're going to start by doing a few tests to see where you are in your education. Now, don't be afraid of these tests. It will just show us where you need to begin." He picked up the phone to make arrangements for the tests.

Reynaldo's eyes surveyed the cluttered room. A framed certificate on the wall showed that Juan Rivera graduated from the University of Texas. There was a picture of a blonde woman and two small children. A poster depicting a bowl of lemons read, "When life gives you lemons, make lemonade."

"Dr. Griffin can do your educational testing this afternoon. Later we'll want to get you into some occupational therapy, a little group therapy, and our chaplain will want to visit with you."

Reynaldo didn't know what a chaplain was, but he didn't ask.

Juan Rivera stood up, so Reynaldo did likewise.

"Do you have any family you'd like me to call?"

"No," Reynaldo replied, looking at the carpeted floor. "They don't have a telephone."

"Oh, Reynaldo . . . one word of advice." He placed an arm around Reynaldo's shoulders, as he started walking with him out the door. "There's a patient out here called Chino. Don't get mixed up with him."

Dr. Benson switched the "on" button and spoke into the recorder with his deliberate and raspy voice. "Thomas Delgado, otherwise known as "Chino" is an 18-year-old Hispanic male, who was admitted to this facility on May 2, 1989. This is the second admission as a condition of his probation from Dallas County. He has been abusing a variety of drugs since the age of ten. Drugs of choice include; crack cocaine, marijuana, and alcohol. He has also used primos extensively and experimented with LSD. He was the acknowledged leader of a Hispanic gang in Dallas. His last arrest on, April 30, 1989, was for aggravated robbery and assault . . ."

"Dr. Benson." Nancy Pitchford, R.N. plunged into his office with a can of anti-perspirant spray in her hand. "This was found in one of the shower stalls in the bathroom. Chino found it. Looks like security has done it again."

The night supervisor's stern indignation was almost amusing to Dr. Benson, who feigned a cough to hide an involuntary smile.

"It's only five o'clock. Aren't you here early, Ms. Pitchford?"

"We have one nurse on vacation this week and one sick, and two new admissions came in this afternoon. This spray can belongs to one of the patients. I think its Murphy's."

"Leave it here," Dr. Benson suggested. "I'll talk to Morrison."

She glared at him for a moment, as if unconvinced that he would handle the situation. Then, she set the can firmly on a corner of the desk, turned abruptly and left.

As usual, Dr. Benson had the strange feeling that she left more than the spray can behind; an inexplicable something that seemed to linger. It was odorless, colorless, and tasteless, and he couldn't put a name to it, but it made him uncomfortable. He wondered if she affected others the same way.

He dialed a number. "Lee, Dr. Benson here. A can of spray deodorant was found in the shower. Check it out . . . who found it? Who do you think? that's right. She thinks it belongs to Ralph Murphy."

An aerosol spray can was just one of a long list of items which were contraband for drug patients. The desperate and clever ones could find ways to get high on the propellant.

Dr. Benson went back to the Dictaphone and pushed the "on" button again. "Reynaldo Garcia is a 15-year-old Hispanic male. He was admitted to this facility on May 14, 1989 as a condition of probation from Bexar County, Texas. Records indicate that . . . at the age of 11, he started sniffing gasoline and paint, and he did that for about two years. He was then introduced to pot and "white crosses", but primarily alcohol. He has been arrested seven times, the first time at the age of 13. He has stolen cars, bicycles, car stereos, fuzz busters, sound equipment, and numerous other items. He is a normal appearing young boy, who talks in a low voice and rarely smiles. There was very little eye contact and he answered most questions with a yes or no answer. He has no apparent thought disorder and his sensorium is clear. He has little insight into his problems. His intelligence is slightly below average and his judgment is somewhat impaired. He is oriented to person, place, and things."

CHAPTER FOUR

Reynaldo bolted upright in bed. Something cold and wet landed in his face, arousing him from a restless sleep. Around him, the other patients were grumbling and shouting obscenities as they, too, were awakened for the day's activities. As his eyes began to focus, he became aware of the plump form of a woman standing over him. She was retrieving the washcloth that had startled him into consciousness. Her broad smile coaxed a slight grin.

"Time to get up," she said. "It's six o'clock. Breakfast will be served in thirty minutes, but not in bed."

Reynaldo had been in the facility three weeks now, and he was gradually adjusting to the early morning calls to breakfast. This was his first time to be awakened by a wet washcloth, but it was certainly a more pleasant experience than being awakened by choking.

He was glad to be away from the detox unit and Nurse Nancy. Just remembering the night supervisor caused a feeling of helplessness to engulf him, like the huge waves that splashed upon the beaches near the Gulf Coast where Reynaldo spent most of his childhood.

But no time to dwell on such gloomy thoughts now, or he would be late for the chow line at the cafeteria. The plump aide had moved on down the row of beds to greet other patients with her wet washcloths and cheerful smile. Reynaldo threw back the covers and touched the cool floor with his bare, brown feet. A hollow feeling in his stomach signaled that he was hungry, so he grabbed his clothes and went to the bathroom to get dressed.

Actually, going to breakfast was one of the rules that he tolerated rather well. Having been deprived of food on a regular basis most of his fifteen years, it seemed really luxurious to be able to eat three meals a day. Many of the patients did not want to eat breakfast and some even refused.

Dr. Benson had explained to him that when the body becomes addicted to drugs, it often rejects food. At first, Reynaldo's appetite was poor and it was very hard for him to get up so early each morning. It was becoming a little easier, and he even liked the food that so many others complained about.

The bathroom was crowded with boys getting out of their green "state issue" pajamas and into their faded and worn out Levis and shirts. A couple of them who were old enough, were shaving with razors that had to be "checked out" from the nurses' station and turned in immediately after use. One of the shavers was Chino, who had just been released to the dormitory the day before.

"That's my shaving soap, Snitch." It was Murphy speaking. The two had been issuing verbal threats toward each other since the spray can incident at detox.

"Better watch out who you call a snitch," Chino sneered and grabbed Murphy's wrist. The aide, Rusty, entered the bathroom and immediately the two broke it up. As Reynaldo walked past them, he overheard Chino threaten Murphy. "I'll get you later." It was then that Reynaldo remembered Juan Rivera's warning about Chino.

He looked at himself in the only full length mirror in the dormitory. Black, sleepy eyes stared back at him as he made an effort to comb down the stubborn lock of hair that always insisted on its own way. His hair was bristly and well below his ears. The Levis were one of two pair he owned. Both pairs were full of tears and holes. These had a hole in the seat, near the hip pocket, and both knees were worn thin. A peeling iron on patch over one knee reminded him of his Aunt Maria. She had applied it there last year. It had been seven months since he had seen her and he wasn't even sure that she was still living in San Antonio.

He slipped the almost toothless comb into his back pocket giving in to the unyielding lock of hair. He did not recognize the similarities in that stubborn lock of hair and himself—wild, defiant, and unwilling to conform to the expectations of others. His eyes rested on the frayed hems of his pants. They had always been too long, and he had actually walked on them until the bottoms were all worn out. He wished he were taller. Here he was, almost sixteen years old and only 5'4". He longed to be tall and "macho". But, his mother was a very tiny woman; less than five feet tall when full grown. That's what Aunt Maria told him.

Rusty stuck his head in the bathroom again and yelled, "Chow time. Everybody out."

Reynaldo stood nervously in the cafeteria line which extended from the serving counter, out into the hallway, and coiled from north to south in a snakelike pattern. He was being jostled about from behind and in front, as well as side to side. A kid he didn't know tried to force his way into the line ahead of him.

"Back to the end of the line, Mike; you know you're not allowed to cut." It was the same aide who had awakened him earlier. Reynaldo learned her name was Beatrice and some of the patients affectionately called her "Auntie Bea". Her voice was soft and pleasant, completely lacking authority.

"I'll do whatever I damn well please, you old bitch," the boy said with contempt. Her round, plump face showed no expression. Reynaldo learned that the aides were often heaped with verbal abuse. It was part of their job to accept that sort of harassment. Their only recourse was to document the behavior in the patient's chart. However, a persistent pattern of unacceptable behavior could result in a period of seclusion.

"Move it!" Rusty ordered. If his voice lacked authority, his size was an effective persuader. Mike moved to the end of the line, muttering obscenities.

Reynaldo was disturbed by the incident because he liked the aide . . . "Auntie Bea". She reminded him of someone from his childhood, but he couldn't remember who.

Most of the tables were filled when Reynaldo finally got his tray of cereal, toast and jelly, and milk.

"Over here, Rey." It was Chino signaling from a table at the far end of the cafeteria. Reynaldo had not forgotten his caseworker's warning, but he doubted that he could get "mixed up" with Chino just by sitting next to him at breakfast. Besides, Chino's offer to "fix him up" with that chick, Carmelita, was very intriguing.

The table was surrounded by a group of Hispanic guys. Reynaldo had noticed how they all seemed to band together, as if part of some unnamed, unorganized club. He wondered if the others had been warned about Chino, too.

"When I was in this place before, there were these two dudes that went over the fence." Chino was saying. "They got all the way to Dallas before they were missed."

"Did they hitch hike?" someone asked.

"A truck driver picked them up just a couple of miles from here." Chino held the group's rapt attention. He had a certain charismatic quality.

"What happened to them?" another asked.

"They got picked up in Dallas for stealing a car, and ended up back here."

"Don't the security people watch the fence all the time?" the fat kid asked.

"They're supposed to," Chino replied, as if an authority on the subject, "but sometimes they sleep on the job."

Reynaldo was distracted from the conversation by the sight of Carmelita, who walked past the group and smiled, teasingly. Reynaldo couldn't tell whether she was flirting with him or Chino, but, probably with Chino.

He ate his breakfast hurriedly, so he wouldn't be late to class. Just before entering the building which contained all the offices and classrooms, a young man in a tropical print shirt and tinted glasses stopped him and held out his hand.

"I'm Owen Matherly, the chaplain." He removed his glasses, revealing light blue, penetrating eyes. "I don't believe I've met you yet, and I like to know all the patients. What is your name?" He smiled in a very friendly manner, as he accompanied Reynaldo into the wide hallway.

"Reynaldo Garcia," Rey responded with downcast eyes.

"Reynaldo, are you on your way to class?"

Rey nodded.

"Well, I won't delay you, now. Who's your caseworker?"

"Juan Rivera."

"Good, I'll make an appointment to see you in my office." He gave him a friendly pat on the shoulder. "I'll see you soon."

So, that was the chaplain. Part of the mystery was solved for Reynaldo, but he still didn't know what the chaplain was supposed to do or why he needed to see him.

CHAPTER FIVE

M iss Glover greeted Reynaldo with her usual cheerfulness. She was not at all like the other teachers Reynaldo remembered. She was young and didn't look very much different from some of the female patients. In fact, she reminded him of Francine, though the teacher wore hardly any make-up. Some of the guys in the dormitory had commented about her being a "good looking chick".

"Are you ready to learn some spelling?" she asked.

He reluctantly nodded his agreement and sat at one of the small desks. As he was opening the book Miss Glover gave him, Carmelita entered the classroom. She was followed by the boy called Mike; the same Mike who tried to cut in the cafeteria line.

"We have two new students today," the teacher said, looking at her class list. "You must be Carmelita Crain and Mike . . . Mike Thornberry. Just sit at any available desk."

There were about a dozen desks in the room, but only seven students. Reynaldo was pleased that Carmelita sat in front of him so he could watch her without turning around. The dude, Mike, sat directly across from Reynaldo. His long, blondish hair was pulled back in a ponytail, exposing rather big ears. Tattooed on his forearm were the numbers "666". Reynaldo knew what that meant. He had been around Satan worshipers before. Miss Glover interrupted his thoughts.

"I'm going to call out a list of words for you to spell. Just do the best you can. I need to determine how much work I need to do with each of you."

Reynaldo shifted uncomfortably. He could barely spell his name. He had not done well on his tests. The education diagnostician had placed him in seventh grade English, math, and social studies. He would also go three times a week to auto mechanics shop and learn a vocation. No one expected him to ever graduate from high school.

Nevertheless, he got out his pencil and paper as did most of the other students. Only Mike didn't respond to the teacher's request.

"This is a classroom, Mike. Get out your pencil and paper," Miss Glover said firmly and evenly. Mike just stared at her, sullenly.

"Get out your paper, or get out of the classroom." She spoke more loudly and firmly. "But, I warn you if you leave the room, I'll report it to your caseworker and caseworkers keep in touch with probation officers." Everyone else sat quietly, waiting to see who would win the battle of wills. Finally, "666" got his paper and pencil out and mumbled, "Fuck teachers."

Miss Glover didn't hear his remark.

We'll start with easy ones. The first word is "window".

Reynaldo wrote slowly, carefully, and probably incorrectly. He made an effort at the first five words she called. Then, he got behind, trying to erase and start over. His fingers and addled brain tried to keep up, but he couldn't do it. Of the twenty words Miss Glover called, he only attempted about half of them, and he was sure most of them were incorrect. He had an almost irresistible urge to crunch his paper into a ball and throw it at the teacher, but he resisted the urge. He didn't want to look stupid to Carmelita. He folded his paper and handed it in with the others. Even Mike turned in a paper and slammed his pencil down on the desk.

"Now, I want you to open your English book and read the short story on page 82. Tomorrow, we will discuss it in class."

Reynaldo tried to read, but it was hard to understand and even harder to concentrate. His eyes kept wandering toward Carmelita. Her dark, thick hair complimented her smooth, olive skin. Chino told him that her mother was Hispanic but her father was a white man. Once, she turned around and caught him looking at her.

"That's all for today class," Miss Glover said. "Tomorrow I'll give you a report on your spelling words and we'll discuss the story."

As the students filed out of the classroom into the hallway, Mike brushed past Reynaldo. "School sucks," he muttered as he headed out the door.

Carmelita stopped to read notices on the bulletin board in the hallway. Reynaldo decided to read them, too.

"They're trying to start a co-ed volleyball team," Carmelita read. "You gonna sign up, Rey?"

Her question caught him off guard, and he blushed. "Are you?"

"No way, Jose," she said emphatically, and looked back at the bulletin board. "Maybe you'd rather play softball. They're having tryouts this afternoon." There was sarcasm in her voice. "What do they think this place is—high school? Seems like they're tryin' to make normal kids out of all us junkies and it ain't gonna happen."

Actually, the idea of playing softball interested Reynaldo. He remembered playing ball in the dirt streets around his Aunt Maria's house, but that seemed long ago, before all his friends started experimenting with drugs.

"How about it?" someone behind him asked. "You want to play ball?" It was Juan Rivera. He put an arm around Rey's shoulder. "Come to my office and let's talk about it."

Reynaldo looked back at Carmelita as Juan steered him toward his office. "You need to participate in some of the recreation we offer while you're here. It will be good for you physically and help you keep your mind off drugs." They entered Juan's office and Reynaldo sat in his usual vinyl chair.

How did you do in class today?" Juan said, abruptly changing the subject.

"Not very good," was the answer. Somehow Rey knew his caseworker had something else on his mind that had nothing to do with softball or school work. He averted Juan's steady gaze by looking past him toward the poster with the bowl of lemons. He still was not sure what it meant about making lemonade out of lemons.

"Rey, I tried to contact your family—your Aunt Maria. I sent a letter to the last address Jim Hagerty had on file. It came back yesterday." Juan laid the letter in front of Reynaldo. It was addressed to Maria Vasquez, 1112 Front St., Brownsville, Texas. MOVED LEFT NO FORWARDING ADDRESS was stamped boldly across the envelope.

Remembering his aunt and the problems he had caused her made tears form in his eyes. She probably never wanted to see him again. He couldn't blame her.

"Mr. Hagerty is investigating the possibility that you might have other relatives somewhere and he's still hoping to find your father."

Reynaldo didn't remember his father at all, though he still carried a faded picture of him standing with his young bride beside an old automobile. He was about a head taller than his wife, slender and dark. Written on the back of the picture were their names—Lupe and Juanita Garcia, 1972. Thinking of his parents was too painful. This time, HE changed the subject.

"Where do they play ball out here?"

Juan understood and smiled. "There's a field out behind the gym. Be there about two o'clock and I bet they'll sign you up."

CHAPTER SIX

Reynaldo's Aunt Maria was thinking about him, but she didn't know where he was. It had been several years since she had seen him.

"Maria Vasquez", the clerk at the counter called above the noise of crying babies and clamoring toddlers. Maria shifted the baby in her arms to redistribute its weight before rising from the uncomfortable metal chair.

"You just sit still," she commanded the young boy who sat next to her. The hyperactive ten-year-old reluctantly returned to his chair. He was the youngest of the Vasquez' six children. The infant she carried was her six week old grandson, the illegitimate child of their sixteen-year-old daughter, Yolanda . . . the child who was born just before Reynaldo came to live with them.

"What is the baby's name? Michelle?" The tall, thin woman behind the thick glasses held a ballpoint pen above a stack of forms.

"Michael Vasquez." She carefully emphasized the first syllable, correcting the woman's pronunciation of the name.

"Address?"

The young grandmother, who looked ten years older than her thirty-five years, dutifully answered her interrogator's questions. She had been through this process before and anticipated each question before it was asked. She was applying for welfare assistance for the baby. The program would buy its formula and pay for medical care. She had first learned about the program when Barbara, her second child was born.

"Is the mother employed?" the clerk asked.

"She's working now. That's why I'm doing this," Maria responded impatiently. "She works at the Dairy Queen about twenty-five hours a week for minimum wages."

"Then, I'll need . . . ."

"Hazel Brown is her supervisor," Maria interrupted the next question.

The forms finally completed, Maria, her son and grandson emerged from the Department of Human Services office into the heat and humidity of a typical summer afternoon in Brownsville. The family had returned to Texas from Louisiana, hoping to work in the orchards. A hard freeze during the winter had damaged the citrus crop and the work had been skimpy. Reuben was working at a gas station, during those times when he was sober, which was less frequently in recent months.

"Edward, mind that red light," she cautioned as they crossed the street where their beat up station wagon was parked. She was anxious to get home and check the mailbox before Reuben got home. She hadn't seen him since he left for work the day before, so she was certain he was drinking again.

She had written a letter to Jim Hagerty, the probation officer in San Antonio. Maybe he would know where Reynaldo was sent. She never had much luck making phone calls. He was always out when she tried and they had no phone for him to return her calls. The family had moved from San Antonio soon after the court placed Reynaldo with a foster family. Once, when they were in Louisiana, she reached Jim Hagerty by phone and learned that Reynaldo had been involved in a robbery. Reuben had forbidden her to try any further contact. He had never treated Reynaldo as their own, and had only agreed to take him, because they had no sons— not until Edward was born. Maria had wanted both her sister's children when their grandmother had to give them up, but Reuben adamantly refused to take the infant. She learned that the girl was adopted by a couple in Dallas, but she never learned their names. They had never mentioned the baby girl again, and she was certain Reynaldo didn't know about his sister. What purpose would it serve for him to know? He would probably never find her.

As Maria approached the small frame house with peeling gray paint, her apprehension mounted. An old brown pickup truck, which belonged to one of Reuben's drinking buddies, was parked in the grassless front yard. She had an impulse to drive on past and keep going—but where? Everyone in the neighborhood was at work, and she knew no one outside the neighborhood. She had left the baby's diapers at home and now he needed changing.

She could hear the men's voices coming from the kitchen as she entered the house. Wanting to avoid a confrontation, she went directly to the bedroom and cautioned Edward to silence with a stern expression. But as soon as she put the baby on the bed to change him, her husband's angry, slurred voice called from the kitchen.

"Maria, come here."

"Just a minute, I'm changing Michael's diaper."

"Now!" he shouted. She heard a chair grate against the linoleum floor and knew he was moving toward the bedroom. Instinctively, she moved away from the baby and pushed Edward behind her. Reuben was mean when he was drunk. Several times he had hit her when drinking. Once, he had caused a bruise that lasted for weeks.

He appeared at the open door, and leaned against the frame with a sneer on his still handsome face. One hand held a white envelope, torn in half. She knew what it was.

"I told you not to try and find that kid." His free hand reached out and overturned a small chair. The baby cried and Edward held onto his mother's skirt and began to whimper. Reuben ripped the envelope into many small pieces and dropped them on the floor.

"I just want to know where he is. I just want to let him know we didn't forget him." Her voice was small and pleading. She tried to put more distance between them but he suddenly grabbed her arm and slapped her hard across the left cheek. Edward cried louder. The other man appeared in the doorway.

"Hey man, don't do that. Let's go get some more beer. I'm buying."

Maria looked at the short, pudgy man through eyes blurred with tears. It was a neighbor from several blocks down the street.

Reuben ignored his friend and grabbed both her wrists. "Do what I say, woman. Don't ever contact that Hagerty again." Abruptly, he dropped her wrists and turned to leave. Hopefully, he would not return that night.

Maria quieted Edward and let him hold a bottle to the baby's mouth. She stooped to gather the pieces of the letter and envelop from the well-worn carpet. The only word that could be salvaged was the San Antonio postmark.

Depositing the pieces in a small wastebasket, she changed the baby's diaper with a new resolve. Someday she would leave her husband, and somehow she would find Reynaldo. Someday. Somehow.

CHAPTER SEVEN

A motley group of male patients was gathered around a muscular blonde guy near the pitcher's mound. "Walt" somebody called him.

"Who can pitch some nice, easy balls?" he asked. "We'll let you guys shag some fly balls. See how good you are in the field." He scanned the group quickly. "Okay, you try it. What's your name?"

"My friends call me Chino. You can call me Thomas. That's what my mama calls me." The few who were counted as his friends and followers laughed. Chino hooked his thumbs in the belt loop of his faded jeans. His chin was tilted upward so that he sort of looked down his nose at Walt, as if challenging the recreation director's authority.

Reynaldo stood a bit apart from the group, with Charles. Most of the boys were there at the insistence of their caseworkers. Participating in sports was part of the prescribed treatment. It was not only considered a healthy activity, but was designed to divert their interest away from drugs. However, organized sports were foreign to most of the patients. One boy seemed to stand out as the exception; a healthy looking white boy with manufactured muscles. Reynaldo had seen him in the cafeteria and in the hallway outside the classroom.

"That's Jock," Charles said. "He's in my horticulture class. His old man is a big time lawyer in Houston." He rolled his eyes in mock adulation and displayed a toothy grin.

Walt asked Jock to hit some fly balls. He faced Chino and everyone else spread out over the field. The first ball went far out in left field and fell to the ground between two boys who moved in slow motion. Reynaldo missed the first one that came whizzing over his head. He quickly decided he was too short for the outfield. The thought angered him and released an intense desire to catch one.

In spite of his shell of indifference, Chino seemed to be enjoying the role of pitcher and Jock had a good, easy swing. He seemed to be a natural athlete.

When the next ball came directly toward Reynaldo, he jumped high, and much to his surprise, caught it. He got an approving look from Walt and several of the boys. More importantly, he caught a smile from Carmelita who was watching from the sidelines with several other girls and attendants.

Then, Walt had Jock pitch while everyone else took a turn at batting. Reynaldo managed to hit a ground ball far out in right field, and it made him feel really good, but when he looked for Carmelita's approval, she was gone.

After their work out on the softball field, Reynaldo was still feeling a glow of satisfaction from having caught one good ball and getting a solid hit with the "big boys". It was a new feeling. One he didn't remember having experienced before.

"Hey, man. You really blasted that ball this afternoon." Charles said. He and Reynaldo were playing poker, with chips, in the day room. The other guys were lounging around the television and smoking. Murphy approached the card table while cautiously looking over his shoulder toward the attendant, Rusty, who was talking on the phone. Murphy held a cigarette pack.

"I have some joints in this pack," he whispered, still watching Rusty. "I'll sell you one for a dollar. Just slip me your money and I'll give you one. You can go in the bathroom and smoke it. Rusty won't know."

Charles looked over his shoulder at the attendant. "Are you serious, man?"

Reynaldo had noticed the others going one by one to the bathroom and wondered what was going on.

"Sure," Murphy whispered. "Francine got it past security in a lipstick case."

Reynaldo had heard the patients discuss various techniques for getting drugs past security inspection. Charles told him some patients had smuggled drugs inside balloons which they swallowed.

Charles pulled a dollar from his pocket and took the hand rolled cigarette Murphy offered. Reynaldo didn't have a dollar. Patients were allowed a few dollars each week to spend at the snack bar, if they were lucky enough to have someone to send money. Charles had just handed over his last dollar.

"I feel a real urge to go to the bathroom," Charles said, putting down his cards. "Come in there in a minute, little buddy. I'll give you a hit."

Reynaldo nervously shuffled cards. Would Rusty catch on? What would happen if they were caught? After a few minutes, he felt the urge to go to the bathroom, too. On the way, he passed by Mike who was sitting alone in a corner and looked like he was in a trance.

A cloud of smoke filled the bathroom. Reynaldo hoped Rusty wouldn't come in, or he would smell it for sure. But, strangely, the familiar odor was missing. Even Chino had one of the "joints". There had been constant tension between Chino and Murphy ever since their stay in detox. Murphy was sure that Chino had reported him for having the deodorant spray can. But no amount of animosity could divert Chino from an opportunity to get "high".

Reynaldo took a long drag off the cigarette Charles offered him. It had a strange taste and the familiar, pungent smell was definitely missing.

"Shit, this must be flea powder," Chino said, flushing the butt down the toilet. "I don't feel nothin".

Charles coughed. "It burns my throat."

"What the fuck IS this stuff?" Chino raged. "You can bet your ass I'll find out."

A loud commotion from the day room prompted a hasty disposal of the cigarette remains. The smokers hurried to learn what was happening.

"Everybody back off, "Rusty was saying, as he hovered near Mike. The wild eyed "acid head" had ripped his shirt off, revealing numerous scars and satanistic symbols on his arms, back and chest. He stood on a chair and clawed at the wall, as if trying to escape from some invisible terror. Pitiful, whimpering sounds emerged from between clenched teeth.

Another attendant, Rusty's night relief, entered the unit and stood transfixed near the nursing station. Rusty shouted to him.

"Call for security and a nurse, then come help me take this character down."

Mike lunged from the chair, ran to the opposite wall, and proceeded to bash his head against it. Before Rusty could restrain him, his nose began to bleed and a small cut appeared on his forehead. Rusty pinned his arms behind him and forced him face down on one of the beds.

It seemed like several minutes before Nurse Nancy arrived with one of the uniformed security men. She uncapped a hypodermic needle and plunged it into Mike's shoulder. "Let's get him to detox, "she ordered.

The men each grabbed an arm and half carried Mike out, with blood still streaming down his face and chest.

Reynaldo had never seen anyone "freak out" before and it unnerved him. He had heard about some scary episodes from taking acid. One of the Banderos claimed to have looked in a mirror while "on a trip" and watched his own face rotting away.

"Man, that Mike really freaked," Charles said, the whites of his eyes standing out in sharp contrast to his dark skin. "I knew a dude in Houston that jumped off a two story building and broke his leg and didn't even know it. Then, he went for a walk straight down the middle of Highway 35."

"What happened then?" Reynaldo asked.

"A highway patrolman picked him up. The last I heard, he was still on acid."

Stimulated by the incident, the boys sat around exchanging "war" stories until Rusty returned and insisted they go to bed.

Murphy's hand rolled cigarettes were practically forgotten by everyone but Chino. He sneered at Murphy as he walked past him. "Where'd you get them lousy flea-powder cigarettes, huh? I'm gonna find out, homeboy."

CHAPTER EIGHT

Miss Glover was actually relieved that Mike was missing from her class. She felt threatened by the boy who was always sullen and openly hostile toward learning. Her efforts to educate these young addicts were mostly unrewarded, but occasionally there would be one whom she could "reach". Reynaldo was that kind of student. Although his IQ was rather low, he seemed to have a real desire to learn, and blossomed under her tutelage. She watched him concentrating on his assignment, a list of questions about facts in Texas history. When puzzled, he would rub his fingers through his unruly hair. When writing answers, he would write very slowly and deliberately, while biting his lower lip. Occasionally, he would glance toward Carmelita, who always sat at the same desk. Although desks were not assigned, the young teacher had observed a tendency of the students to sit exclusively at their original desks. She surmised that, having "staked their claim", it was comforting to return to the same spot.

After class, as Reynaldo turned in his paper, she took the opportunity to offer some words of encouragement as she often did.

"You're doing great, Rey. The essay you turned in yesterday was very good. I'm just going to make a few corrections, and I'll give it back to you tomorrow."

Rey returned her smile. Writing the essay had been difficult. She had given the students a title only and asked each of them to write two paragraphs about "The Rest of My Life". How could he know about the rest of his life? Actually, he tried not to think beyond tomorrow, but the assignment forced him to think about it. He had done a bit of day dreaming and imagined himself as a social worker, like Juan. Then, he imagined himself and Carmelita in that framed picture in Juan's office, with two kids. That's what he wrote about, but he didn't name Carmelita.

In the hall, he stopped near the bulletin board to talk with Carmelita for a few minutes, before going to the chaplain's office. Her attitude toward the facility had softened somewhat since he first talked to her, several weeks ago.

"There's going to be a talent show, "she said, reading a prominent notice on the bulletin board. "You gonna be in it, Rey?"

"Nah, I ain't got no talent. Are you?"

"No way, Jose. I was on a stage once when I was five years old. I was supposed to sing "God Bless America" and I forgot the words. I started crying and ran off the stage." She had a faraway look in her eyes. "Funny, I hadn't thought of that before. I guess I'd forgotten about it."

The corners of her thin lips, covered with pink lip gloss, formed a weak smile. Reynaldo wondered how that lip gloss would taste. The soft curves beneath her yellow T-shirt had not gone unnoticed. He longed to touch her, but instead he said, "I'll see you later, I have an appointment with the chaplain."

As he passed by the restroom, he saw Murphy go inside. Chino and two of his buddies rounded the corner and looked both ways down the hall. Chino grabbed Rey's arm and instructed him to stay there and warn them if he saw anybody coming. The three entered the restroom behind Murphy. Rey stood in his tracks, afraid to move, not wanting to cross Chino.

Rey heard the shuffling of feet, a series of dull thuds and several loud grunts and groans. Then, silence.

Murphy's attackers emerged from the restroom, and two of them fled quickly around the corner. Chino paused long enough to whisper. "If anybody asks, you ain't seen nothing." Then, he too, disappeared around the corner. The long hallway was empty and Reynaldo's feet felt like they were set in concrete. He didn't know whether to go in the restroom or go on to his appointment with the chaplain and pretend he didn't see anything. But, what if Murphy was dead or dying? The only thing he was sure about was that he didn't want to be one of Chino's victims.

The sound of low moans from the restroom interrupted his thoughts and he decided to go in. Murphy was trying to get up off the floor. He was supporting his weight on one knee and one hand, while his forehead rested in the other hand. Blood dripped onto the floor from his nose and battered lips. Reynaldo couldn't see his eyes.

"I'll go find someone to help you." He was uncertain whether Murphy even heard him.

Leaving the restroom, he decided to go directly to the chaplain's office, since he was already late. Owen Matherly would know what to do.

The slightly balding chaplain greeted Reynaldo with his usual cheerfulness. "Hey, it's good to see you again." He shook Reynaldo's hand. "Is something wrong?"

"Mr. Matherly, I just came from the restroom. Murphy is in there, bleeding. He had an accident." The words tumbled out.

The chaplain looked puzzled. "What kind of accident?"

Reynaldo avoided the chaplain's eyes. "I don't know. I just found him there, and told him I'd find someone to help him."

"I'll call security and let them handle it." Owen Matherly picked up the phone and pushed several buttons . . . "Then, we can talk." After relaying the scanty information to Lee Morrison, he settled down in the chair behind the desk and signaled Rey to sit. "Someone from security and a nurse are on their way. They'll take care of him."

He paused a minute, studying Rey, "You don't know what happened, huh?"

"No." Rey lied. He squirmed in his chair and avoided eye contact.

Owen Matherly was sure he knew more than he was telling, but it wasn't his job to put pressure on him. It was his job to get to know him better and help him find solutions for his problems.

"Tell me about your family, Rey." The chaplain already knew just about everything about him, because he had read his social history, but he wanted Rey to talk. "You lived with your aunt after your mother died?" He leaned back in his chair, propped his feet on a corner of the desk, and folded his hands under his chin.

"Yes." Reynaldo studied the room. The walls on two sides were lined with books. A big Bible lay open on the desk.

Matherly waited, but there was no other response. This may be tough, he thought.

"Did you have any brothers or sisters?"

"No, just my cousins. My mother died when I was two."

"Do you remember her?"

"Sometimes . . . do you want to see a picture of her?" For the first time since he came into the room, he looked directly at the chaplain.

"Sure," Matherly said, removing his feet from the desk. He seemed very interested.

Reynaldo opened the worn out billfold and handed it across the desk.

"Ah. She's pretty and looks so young. Is this your father?"

"Yes. Aunt Maria said he went to West Texas to find a job in the oil fields and she never heard from him again. He was supposed to come back to get me, but he never came."

The chaplain returned the billfold, then stood up and walked to the window. "Well, Rey, it seems life hasn't been very good to you, so far. Let's see, how old are you now? Sixteen?" He turned and looked at the boy in the chair.

"Almost." Rey wondered what was coming next.

"How old do you want to be?"

Rey was puzzled. Does he mean, right now?

"Do you want to live another year? Five years? Fifty years?"

This line of questioning was unexpected and Rey didn't know how to answer.

The chaplain walked back to the desk and sat on the edge and smiled. "Most people want to live forever, but no one knows how long his life will be. I just want you to know I'd like to help you find the best way to live your life. I want to be your friend." He stood up again. "Did you ever go to church, Rey?"

Rey hesitated. He couldn't count the time he and the Banderos broke into three churches in one night and stole all their sound equipment.

"No, my Aunt Maria used to go sometime."

"I haven't seen you at any of the chapel services yet. Will you come Sunday morning?"

Rey knew about the chapel services. In fact, Charles had gone several times, but Rey hadn't wanted to go. He had always imagined church to be a place for good people. What could God do with a bunch of drug addicts?

As if reading his thoughts, Matherly said, "God loves drug addicts, too." He walked toward the door, dismissing Rey.

Reynaldo got up to leave, promising to attend the chapel service with Charles.

"You still playing softball?" the chaplain asked.

Reynaldo smiled and nodded.

"I watched you guys work out last week and you're pretty good, Rey. Keep it up." The chaplain pointed one thumb in the air as a parting gesture.

Rey walked past the restroom on his way back to the dorm and saw a few drops of blood in the hallway. He wondered how badly Murphy was hurt.

CHAPTER NINE

The boys gathering for softball practice were buzzing about Murphy's "accident". The word had spread rapidly. On their way to the ball field Charles and Jock had seen him being half-carried to detox by a security guard and a nurse.

"He looked bad, man," Charles said, his big eyes bulging. "I bet I know who worked him over." He picked up a bat and took a practice swing. "He looked like he tangled with one of these." He assumed a batting stance and wiggled his tail.

Reynaldo made no comment. Murphy could tell what happened in the restroom, if he wanted to, but Reynaldo was determined to say nothing. He wondered if Chino and his henchmen would show up for ball practice. Walt had announced last week that they might have a real game with a team of "straight" guys from town. The idea of some real competition seemed to capture the interest of Walt's team which called themselves the "Abusers".

The boys had already spread out in the field for practice with Jock on the pitcher's mound when Chino showed up; acting as though nothing had happened.

"Chino, grab a bat and hit some balls to the infield." Walt shouted.

There were not enough players to field two teams, so they just played drills. Occasionally, they were able to recruit enough staff members to play a real game.

Chino choked up on the bat, and bent forward from the waist. Jock did a wind up like one of the pros. Reynaldo, at short stop, heard the crack of the bat and then, nothing.

When he opened his eyes again, he was lying on a bed in a room that looked vaguely familiar, but slightly out of focus. Dr. Benson was leaning over him; with a small light which he shined into Rey's eyes—first the right, then the left. With the edge of his hand he brushed Rey's hair from his forehead.

"You've got quite a lump there, Rey . . . and a slight concussion, but you'll be alright." He turned toward the nurse beside him. "Give him Tylenol if he develops a headache. He'll probably sleep well tonight . . . but our other patient might need a sedative."

Reynaldo could hardly keep his eyes open, but he looked toward the next bed where the patient had an arm in a sling and his head swathed in bandages. Reynaldo knew it had to be Murphy. Low moans verified his suspicion that Murphy was rather badly hurt. They were roommates in one of the isolation rooms at detox. Having identified his surroundings, Reynaldo drifted back into a semi-conscious state.

He had no idea how much later it was when he heard voices in the room and opened his eyes just enough to let in a little light. His eyelids felt so heavy.

"You're feeling pretty bad, huh, Murphy? Did you ever think that you might deserve what you got?" It was Nurse Nancy. Murphy mumbled something Rey didn't understand.

"You see this hypodermic needle, Murphy? Do you know what this is?" Rey could barely discern her white, ghostly form through eyes that struggled to open.

"This is Demerol, Murphy. Demerol. Think how good it would make you feel, but I don't think you can have it, Murphy. I don't think you deserve to feel good."

"Give me that needle, bitch," Murphy said, through bruised swollen lips.

Reynaldo forced his eyes open as he became aware of Murphy's sudden lunge from his bed. He watched as Murphy used his free hand to grab her arm that held the needle. As the needle fell to the floor,

Murphy swung at the nurse with his one good arm and sent her sprawling across the room, knocking over a chair. The noise brought the aide, Larry McBride, rushing into the room. He quickly assessed the situation and grabbed Murphy, who was fumbling around for the fallen needle. Nurse Nancy, stunned by the fall, and shocked by Murphy's sudden violence, struggled slowly to her feet.

"Are you okay?" McBride asked her, with little apparent concern.

"Put him in lock-up," she screamed through clenched teeth.

McBride pushed Murphy out of the room and herded him away, down the hall. Only then did the nurse seem to acknowledge Reynaldo's presence in the room. She stared at him for a long moment while massaging her shoulder. Then, she turned out the light, plunging the room in darkness, and left.

Reynaldo slept through most of the next day, waking long enough to sip some juice through a straw and go to the bathroom. A sleepy-eyed, tousle haired image blinked back at him from the bathroom mirror. A big red and purple lump adorned his forehead just above the right eyebrow. It throbbed with a dull pain. Suddenly he recalled the incident that caused the lump. But, who hit the ball? He couldn't remember.

When he returned to his bed on shaky legs, Dr. Benson was waiting for him.

"Are you feeling better, Rey?"

Rey nodded, as he gratefully climbed back into the bed.

"Have you been nauseated?"

"No, just sleepy."

"You'll be over that sleepiness by tomorrow, I think, but that knot on your noggin will probably take a few more days."

Dr. Benson sat down on the edge of the bed and leaned in closer, appearing ill-at-ease.

"Rey, did you see what went on in here last night? Between Murphy and Ms. Pitchford?"

Reynaldo hesitated a moment, reviewing the incident as it registered in his memory. "Yes," he answered, softly.

Dr. Benson hesitated. "Well, I won't bother you with it now, but when you're better, I want you to tell me about what you saw."

Reynaldo hesitated, "Okay."

As Dr. Benson left the room with the nurse, Reynaldo heard him tell her, "Nancy Pitchford will be off work for a few days. Duffy will be on as night supervisor."

Reynaldo's eyes focused on a big round clock on the opposite wall . . . 6:30 . . . while he was trying to decide whether it was morning or evening, Chino stuck his head through the doorway.

"Hey, man, how you doin?" He asked in a hoarse whisper. Then, he entered the room, slyly, looking back over his shoulder. Nearing the bed, he said "I'm sorry that ball went right for you head. I didn't aim it that way, honest." Again, he looked back toward the door.

Rey couldn't believe this guy was in his room. What was he doing here? Who let him in?

"Hey, I brought someone to see you." He went back to the open door and motioned to someone. Carmelita followed him back into the room, looking nervous, and Chino pulled the door shut. "Don't worry, they're busy admitting a patient and won't be checking on anyone for a while. He smiled an unfriendly smile, displaying his chipped tooth. "Don't worry, punk, me and McBride are just like this." He held up two crossed fingers. Slipping out the door, he said, "Have fun."

Reynaldo hadn't said a word through the whole scenario. Trying to figure out what was going on was too taxing for his tired, injured brain. Carmelita stood beside his bed, looking down at him. Her frosty pink lips formed a seductive smile.

"I was worried about you. Chino told me he could get me in to see you, because he and Larry McBride are friends . . . whatever that means." She shrugged and sat on the edge of the bed.

Rey finally found his voice. "We'll be in trouble if they find you here."

"Chino said the side door would be unlocked. I can slip out that way."

Reynaldo tried to sit up, but he felt dizzy and slid back down on his pillow.

"Are you hurt badly?" Carmelita looked concerned.

"Not too bad." He really wanted to evoke her sympathy. It wouldn't hurt to stretch the truth a little. "I'll be out of here in a few days, but I don't know if I can play ball anymore."

"Oh, I hope you can, you really like it, don't you?"

He nodded in agreement. He really wanted to talk to this girl, but he didn't know what to say, and he was nervous about her being in the room. He didn't want her to be in seclusion for breaking the rules, and he didn't trust Chino's motives in bringing her there.

A noise in the hallway prompted Carmelita to stand and look nervously toward the door. "I better get out of here," she whispered, and quickly leaned over and touched Reynaldo's lips with her own. In a moment, she was out the door and gone.

Reynaldo ran his tongue around his lips, savoring the taste of pink lipstick. He drifted back into sleep, relishing the looks, taste, and scent of Carmelita.

CHAPTER TEN

The second morning, following Reynaldo's accident, he awoke feeling much better. He was more alert, and hungry. His eyes focused on the empty bed next to him and he remembered Dr. Benson's remarks about the incident between Murphy and Nurse Nancy.

Evidently, Murphy had not divulged the cause of his "accident" in the restroom. Otherwise, Chino and his friends would be in seclusion. It seemed strange that Murphy wouldn't tell. Reynaldo wondered why.

After he had eaten a breakfast of oatmeal and toast, while sitting on the edge of the bed, Dr. Benson came in.

"Rey, how're you feeling this morning?" He peered closely at the lump of Rey's forehead. "That's looking better. It's gone down some, but still a psychedelic purple." He moved to the foot of the bed. "Rey" he began, as he put on his serious expression, accenting the deep, vertical crease between his eyes. "The staff is having a meeting this morning. If you feel up to it, we'd like you to come tell us what you saw and heard in here the night before last."

Reynaldo looked up at the doctor whom he had learned to like and respect. "Okay." He supposed he could do that without mentioning Chino's name.

Juan Rivera entered the staff meeting a few minutes late, as usual. He had been delayed by a phone call from Jim Hagerty, Reynaldo's probation officer. There was a possibility that Reynaldo had a grandmother living in El Paso. He was checking on it, but, of course, he wouldn't mention it to

Reynaldo until he was certain. He wouldn't want to build up his hopes, only to disappoint him.

The long table was surrounded by key staff members who met periodically to review a list of patients. Dr. William Lupenski, head psychologist, directed the meetings. He had a reddish beard which he stroked while looking over some papers laid out in front of him.

"Our first case is Walter Newhouse III, otherwise known as Jock. He's been here . . . five months, almost. How's he doing with you, Steve?" The questions were directed to a young caseworker who looked not much older than the patients.

"He's playing it cool. Doing and saying all the right things, but I think he's manipulating us just like he manipulated his parents."

"What about his parents? Have you talked with them lately?"

Jock's caseworker shook his head. "They're hard to find. Mr. Newhouse and his new bride have been on an extended cruise. Jock's mother is at a health spa somewhere in Arizona. The only persons I ever talk to are the housekeepers."

"If either of them can settle down for a week, why don't we send Jock on a furlough and see how he does?"

The caseworker nodded his assent. "I'll work on it."

"Just don't send him home till after our ballgame next week." It was Walt. Everyone chuckled.

"The next case is Charles Knotts. Charles has been here since the middle of May, a little over three months. Cathy, he's on your caseload, right?"

Cathy, thirtyish, was the only female social worker on the staff. Most of the female patients were hers, and a few boys. Charles was one of them, and one of her most distressing problems. The friendly, amiable black boy was a very likeable sort, and bright.

"He's done very well, as far as I'm concerned, and I think he would continue to do well in a very structured environment, but I'm afraid he can't handle the outside."

"Isn't he the one with ten brothers and sisters?" Walt asked.

Cathy, who wore black rimmed glasses and a severe hairdo, frowned. "Yes. His father was killed in a gun fight outside a juke-joint, and his mother has struggled to make a living for the kids. Three of his brothers are in prison and one of his sisters. I just don't think he'll make it if he has to go back to that environment."

"He's eighteen, isn't he? Where is he academically?" Dr. Lupenski asked.

Dr. Griffin, the diagnostician, answered. "He's close to a high school diploma. ; one more English and one more math course is all he needs. "I've made inquiries into the possibility of getting him some scholarships for college through the United Negro College Fund as well as a Pell Grant."

"Follow up on that, Cathy," Dr. Lupenski suggested. "We certainly need to keep him here until we can make satisfactory discharge plans . . . Carmelita Crain is our next problem. I think Luke Benson has a report on her."

Dr. Benson glanced around the table and addressed the group while remaining in his seat. "As most of you know, Carmelita just returned from a week furlough a little more than two months ago. She got back with her same old group of friends in Dallas and came back under the influence of cocaine. She also came back pregnant. This was just confirmed a couple of days ago."

Cathy's fist came down on the table. "Oh, how could she do this? I was making some progress with her, I thought. Just before she came here, she learned she was adopted as an infant. That information hit her pretty hard, but we've been working through that.

"That girl has a real identity problem. Her adopted mother is Mexican and her father is Caucasian, so she hasn't felt a part of either culture.

"What will we do now, Dr. Benson?"

"Well, obviously, any recommendations we make will have to include the baby."

"What about an abortion? Did she mention that?" asked the director of nursing services.

"She seems pleased with the idea of having a baby, which shows her level of immaturity. 'At least, I'll have someone of my own,' she said. Besides, by the time she could be convinced, it would probably be too late."

"If she has that attitude, she might not be convinced to give it up for adoption, either." Cathy remarked, shaking her head in frustration.

"Talk to her, Cathy, and see if you can reason with her. If you need any help, send her to me . . . anymore discussion about Carmelita?" Dr. Lupenski asked.

Juan Rivera was aware that Reynaldo liked this girl, Carmelita, and wondered how this news would affect him.

"Now, we need to discuss Ralph Murphy. He wasn't on our schedule for review, but a couple of incidents this week with Murphy as the main character, moved him up on our list. Most of you probably know about the "accident" in the restroom, in this building. It seemed pretty obvious that someone worked him over. Did he ever say who it was, Luke?"

"Negative. I have a strong suspicion that Murphy plans to retaliate, if we let him stay. I think this young fellow is a time bomb about to explode.

"There was an incident in detox night before last between Murphy and the night supervisor. Reynaldo Garcia was in the room at the time, with a slight concussion. He's waiting outside to come in and tell us what happened."

"Okay, bring him in." Lupenski walked to a side table and refilled his mug of coffee.

Reynaldo was almost as nervous about entering the staff meeting as he had been on his arrival at the facility. He still felt a little weak from two days in bed. Some of the faces around the table were unfamiliar, but spotting Juan Rivera in the group made him feel more comfortable.

"Sit over here, Rey," Dr. Benson said, pointing to a chair against the wall.

"Rey, will you please tell us exactly what you remember from two nights ago when Ralph Murphy was in the same room with you at detox?"

All eyes were on him. He swallowed and cast his eyes at the brown tweed carpet. "Uh, I had been sleeping a lot, and the nurse probably thought I was asleep."

"Which nurse, Rey? The night supervisor, Mrs. Pitchford?" Dr. Benson prompted.

"Yes, she had a needle in her hand, and asked Murphy if he wanted it. He mumbled something I didn't understand. She uh . . . she told him it was Demerol, and she said, 'this sure would make you feel good', or something like that." Rey looked up and all eyes were still riveted on him. He looked over their heads toward the ceiling.

"What happened then?" Dr. Benson asked.

"She told him he couldn't have it. That he didn't deserve to feel good . . . that he probably deserved what he got. Then, uh . . . I heard Murphy say, 'Give me that'. He jumped out of bed and grabbed her arm. I heard the needle hit the floor. Then, I guess he pushed her, or hit her. She fell over the furniture." Reynaldo paused. "Then, someone came in and grabbed Murphy and took him out."

"Larry McBride?"

"Yes, I think so. The nurse must have got up by herself. Then, I guess she left. I shut my eyes and pretended to be asleep."

There was silence and Dr. Lupenski said, "Does anyone have any questions?"

"Rey, do you know what happened to Murphy in the restroom?" asked Juan Rivera.

The question hit hard. He had been fearful that someone would ask him point blank, but he was more fearful of Chino.

"No," he lied.

"Alright, you can go." Dr. Lupenski dismissed him. "Thanks for coming in."

Reynaldo left the room quickly and started toward the auto mechanics building for his class. Mixed emotions set his heart throbbing. He felt good about his part in what he hoped would be the dismissal of Nurse Nancy. But, he felt real bad about lying to Juan Rivera.

CHAPTER ELEVEN

The auto mechanics shop was bustling with activity when Reynaldo arrived about ten minutes late. Two cars were parked inside. Several of the students were occupied putting mag wheels on a vintage Camaro. A late model Buick Riviera had the hood raised as the burly instructor pointed out features of the modified engine to the group of students around the vehicle. No one seemed to notice him as he joined the circle. Only Chino looked at him, with that familiar smirk on his face.

"How'd you make out with Carmelita?" he whispered. Reynaldo ignored him as the instructor, Earl Mason, led them to the Camaro, and raised the hood, continuing his lecture on the difference in fuel systems.

The half dozen boys in the shop were then given specific assignments to carry out as Mason circulated among them, offering supervision.

"Reynaldo, start the engine in the Buick," Mason instructed. Reynaldo opened the door and entered the plush interior and turned the ignition key. He noticed a small brass nameplate affixed to the dashboard, above the digital clock-L. McBride. Must be Larry McBride of detox, he thought. Most of the vehicles were brought to the shop by staff members who were charged for parts, but not for labor. As he emerged from the car, he noticed Chino at the rear of the vehicle, on his knees. He saw him reach underneath the left fender and remove something which he quickly stuffed into his back pocket, while looking furtively toward the instructor's back. He returned Reynaldo's stare, as if challenging him to silence. Reynaldo didn't see what Chino put in his pocket, but he was sure it was contraband.

Suddenly, he remembered Chino's statement upon delivering Carmelita to his room at detox . . . "Don't worry . . . me and McBride is just like this."

A few minutes later, when Reynaldo was in the supply closet getting transmission oil, Chino met him at the door.

"Okay, runt, I know you saw me, but you better keep quiet. I know you can do it. You did just right about the Murphy thing," he said, applying a weak fist to Reynaldo's chin. "Besides, if you ever tell, remember, you had Carmelita in your room. Both of you could be in trouble over that." Giving Reynaldo his most sinister look, he walked away.

On his way back to the dorm after classes, Reynaldo was deep in thought. He was beginning to understand the nature of Chino's friendship with McBride. The aide was supplying him with drugs. He almost collided with Carmelita as she hurried toward the girls' dorm.

"Are you going to the talent show tonight?"

"Yeah, I guess so."

"I'll see you there," she said, hurrying on.

His thoughts immediately returned to Chino, Larry McBride, and detox. He wondered what would happen if the staff learned about Carmelita being in his room, even though Chino was responsible. Would Chino ever be caught in his devious behavior? Reynaldo longed to tell Juan Rivera everything he knew about Chino, but he was afraid. Afraid he would be attacked by Chino and his friends just like Murphy. Remembering Murphy, he thought of Nurse Nancy. He wondered what would happen next.

Drs. Lupenski and Benson waited in the former's office for the arrival of Nancy Pitchford. The two had agreed that Luther Benson would reiterate the problems leading to her suspension and Dr. Lupenski would tell her of their decision to suspend her for six weeks without pay. He was the type who enjoyed having the last word.

At her own request, she had been absent from her job for the past three days, on sick leave. Now, the time of reckoning had come. The R.N., who had been employed by the facility less than a year, was subject to suspension because of the incident involving Ralph Murray. There had been other incidents since her employment, but usually subtle in nature. It had been obvious since her arrival there that she was disliked and not trusted by patients and staff.

A faint knocking on the door preceded her entrance. The formidable nurse appeared smaller somehow. Her face was expressionless and her drill sergeant demeanor was missing. She was dressed in a pair of khaki slacks and a plaid blouse. It was the first time; Dr. Benson had seen her in anything but a nurse's uniform.

Dr. Lupenski cleared his throat and broke the silence. "Ms. Pitchford, I believe you know why we've called you in this morning." She still did not speak.

"Please, sit down." Dr. Benson indicated a chair. She complied.

"I . . . ." she began, and then swallowed, appearing to be on the verge of tears.

"Ms. Pitchford, do you have anything to add to what we've already heard about the events of August sixth in the detox unit? You know I'm speaking of the incident involving Ralph Murphy."

She gripped the chair arms until her knuckles turned white. A look of hate and anger flashed in her eyes. "They killed my daughter. They shot her full of heroin. She went into a coma and died." She came out of the chair and began pacing the floor. Her voice rose in volume and pitch, as her inquisitors watched in shocked silence.

"She was only fifteen . . . fifteen . . . do you hear me?" She screamed at them. "She was all I had." Her arms were crossed against her chest and she rubbed her arms as she continued pacing. "She was all I had-do you understand me? They killed her. I hate them." She gasped, "I hate every one of these dope heads . . ." She dropped back into the chair and sobbed with her face buried in the palms of her hands. Her body shuddered as the sobbing continued.

Dr. Benson and Lupenski looked at each other, uncertain what their next course should be. This scenario was unexpected. Dr. Benson moved toward the nurse and placed a big hand on her shoulder. She shook loose from his gesture of concern.

"Don't pretend you care," she said hoarsely. "You deceive yourselves thinking you can cure these hoodlums. They're the scum of the earth and they hurt and kill everyone they touch. You might as well give them all a lethal dose of drugs and be done with them. Let them all die, like my daughter. My Cindy . . . my Cindy . . ." she continued shaking with sobs, as rivulets of tears stained both cheeks.

It seemed obvious that a six week suspension was out of the question. The tormented woman who crumpled before them could not return to the facility. Lupenski picked up the phone to call the Crestview Clinic, a private treatment center for the emotionally disturbed.

CHAPTER TWELVE

Florencia Garcia replaced the telephone on the receiver and hastily removed a pot from the stove, burning her finger in the process. The stinging burn momentarily diverted her attention from the phone call. A Mr. Hagerty had just informed her that her grandson, Reynaldo, was now living in a drug center in east Texas. The news stirred up turmoil of emotions. For years, she had tried to learn the whereabouts of Reynaldo and his younger sister. When poor Juanita was killed in an accident soon after the girl was born, Florencia had taken the children to her home in Mexico for several months, but it became impossible for her to care for them. She and her husband were already old and Alonso soon died of a heart attack. Florencia was left to seek out a living for herself.

Memories from long ago crowded her mind as she stirred the scorched custard, trying to salvage part of it for Dr. Bergman's dinner. She looked up at the round wall clock. It was already 5:30 and the doctor liked his dinner promptly at six. She hastened to prepare the chicken for the oven, but she could not stop the flood of memories. She had left the children in a Mexico City orphanage for about three months before rumors of abuse caused her to contact Juanita's only sister, Maria, to take the children. Maria's husband, Reuben, refused to take the infant, so a lawyer for whom Florencia worked, arranged for a Texas couple to take the one year old girl. The couple had a Caucasian name which Florencia had carefully printed on a yellowed page in a little black notebook she kept . . . CRAIN. The lawyer had since died, and she had no idea where the Crain family lived.

Everything she needed to remember was written in her little notebook . . . birthdays, death dates, and the address of her one son who had a more or less permanent address. He worked for a cattle ranch in New Mexico, but never married. Four other sons and their families were itinerant farm laborers and moved frequently from state to state, harvesting crops. Florencia still grieved about her son, Lupe. He disappeared soon after Maria's death and wasn't heard from again. She was certain that he was dead too.

Florencia closed the oven door and reminded herself to pay attention to her cooking. Dr. Bergman didn't like his food overcooked. She dipped a finger in the egg custard and licked the sugary mixture to determine if it was too scorched to serve. The portion in the center seemed okay. The sound of the doctor's car pulling into the garage startled her. He was twenty minutes earlier than usual.

The tall, paunchy Dr. Bergman was a man in his late sixties, but Florencia thought he looked younger. She had been his housekeeper ever since his wife died twelve years ago. He was a semi-retired optometrist, but still saw a few patients at an El Paso clinic in the afternoons. Most mornings he worked outdoors in the flower and vegetable gardens of the three acre estate.

"Flora is my dinner ready?" he asked wearily. It was obvious the doctor was not in a particularly good humor. His housekeeper was aware that an old knee injury was giving him some misery. She had hoped to see him a bit more cheerful because of the question she wished to ask.

"In just a minute, Dr. Bergman-soon as I warm these fresh green beans." She glanced at the doctor surreptitiously as he headed toward the den, the evening newspaper folded under his arm. She tried to gauge whether her initial assessment of his mood was accurate. If so, she best wait until morning for any serious conversation. The doctor usually awoke with a pleasant outlook on life. Flora had learned to read his moods with considerable accuracy and had more than once used them to her advantage.

"Dinner's ready, Dr. Bergman." She set the platter of sizzling chicken and side dishes of brown rice and green beans near one end of the long dinner table where he always took his meals. It was just a habit that never changed. Sometimes they conversed through the open kitchen door, but usually, the doctor would read as he ate. This evening he surprised her by calling her into the dining room. He pulled a chair away from the table, inviting her to sit down.

"Flora," he began, putting down his fork, "I saw Dr. Franks today about my knee. He thinks I need surgery to remove some cartilage. I've got to get someone to come help Rico with the yard work. I won't be able to do it anymore. Do you know anyone who wants a little part time work?"

This unexpected question seemed like the perfect opportunity to present her request concerning her grandson. She wouldn't wait until morning. "How about a teenage boy?"

"That might be alright." Dr. Bergman fingered the fork beside his plate. "Do you know someone?"

Florencia fidgeted nervously in the high backed chair. "Yes, my grandson."

Dr. Bergman looked directly at her for the first time since he arrived home. "I didn't know you had a grandson in El Paso."

Florencia fidgeted again. "He's in a hospital in east Texas, and he has no place to go. Can he come live with me, Dr. Bergman?" She blurted the question, while smoothing the wrinkles in her soiled apron.

What kind of hospital?"

Florencia hesitated, but she knew she could not lie to her employer. "A hospital for teenagers with drug problems; this is my grandson whose mother died when he was two. I kept him and his baby sister for a while, but I couldn't take care of them, so I had to give them up." The whole story poured from her lips while the doctor listened patiently. "I could fix up that extra bedroom in the guest house for him," she offered hopefully.

"You know how I feel about drugs," he said in reproof. "Did I smell custard when I came in?"

She got up quickly and returned to the kitchen, biting her lip to keep from crying. It seemed she should have waited until morning.

CHAPTER THIRTEEN

Reynaldo entered the dormitory just as Auntie Bea was distributing mail to some of the patients. Charles was ripping open a long white envelope.

"Did I get anything?" Reynaldo asked hopefully.

Auntie Bea looked at him with compassion and rested a flabby arm around his shoulders. "No, Rey not this time. Maybe tomorrow."

She smiled sweetly, and again, just for a brief moment, Rey sensed a certain familiarity. The sensation was so vague and so brief; it evaporated like a wisp of smoke. He didn't expect to get any mail, but still, he hoped. Maybe his Aunt Maria didn't know he was here, but he knew she could find out by contacting Jim Hagerty.

Charles sat on the edge of his bed reading the letter. His thick lips silently mouthed the words. A frown formed on his ebony face.

"Bad news?" Rey asked his friend.

"My mother is in the hospital. She had a stroke." He glanced at Rey, then back at the message scribbled on notebook paper. "This letter is from my sister."

He crumpled the paper and threw it on the floor, shaking his head slowly. "Man, I need to be there. There ain't no one to look after my brothers and sisters. Tosha is the oldest one at home and she's only twelve."

"Talk to your caseworker, maybe she'll let you out."

"No way, I've got charges against me. If I get out of here early, I'll probably go to jail."

Not knowing what else to say, Rey went to his own bed to rest a few minutes before supper time. He picked up the book Miss Glover asked him to read. In two weeks he must write a report on "The Last of the Mohicans". She told him this was equal to a ninth grade assignment and he was determined to do well.

A kid named Pete strummed his guitar from the bed in the far corner of the room. He would be one of the acts in tonight's talent show. Rey found it impossible to concentrate on the adventures of Natty Bumpo. He was thinking of Chino and wondering about his "connection" with Larry McBride. What did McBride plant under his car fender and why? Chino couldn't have very much money, or could he? Rey recalled seeing Francine slipping him some money in the cafeteria the day before yesterday. He'd wondered at the time what was going on.

Rey tried to remember how long it had been since his last "high". Four months? Five? . . . a long time . . . too long. Such thoughts breeded an almost overwhelming desire for drugs. In an effort to suppress such thoughts, he put down his book and went to the day room where most of the others were watching TV until time for the evening meal.

There, Chino sat among the others, nonchalantly watching "Family Feud" as if everything was "cool". With a glance, he dared Reynaldo to squeal on him and his unscrupulous supplier.

The intermittent conversation around the TV soon focused on the talent show. "I can't wait to see Francine's act," the fat boy said, obviously excited. "She's gonna dance."

The metal chairs lined up on the gymnasium floor filled up slowly as many of the patients lingered in groups outside the building until the staff told them sternly to go inside and be seated. Chino was the last one to take a seat, prodded by Miss Glover. Most of the staff was present for the talent show, a sure indication that it was an important event. Performances such as this were considered a tool to boost the participants' self-esteem and encourage new avenues of expression.

Rey sat next to Charles who still seemed distracted by the news from home. Rey looked around for Carmelita and spotted her near the far end of the row behind him. She had been acting strangely, as if trying to avoid him. He wondered how she could have changed so quickly. He was puzzled and hurt.

An ear shattering squelch from the PA system interrupted his thoughts. Dr. Lupenski was adjusting the microphone to accommodate his short, sturdy body. The audience was restless and noisy; refusing to quiet down for several minutes after the supervisor began his opening remarks.

"Students . . . ." The young drug offenders were alternately referred to as patients, clients, or students. There was a lengthy pause, and then he began again, but louder, as the noise continued. "Students, I understand your excitement this evening. This is a rare occasion and perhaps we should have this type of event more frequently."

What he didn't understand, at the moment, was that many of the "students" were already hyper from sniffing "coke". Cocaine purchased from Chino who purchased it from Larry McBride with money he had been collecting for weeks. Rey's eyes scanned the crowd and he could pick out those who were "high". He was filled with a conflicting mixture of disgust and envy. The unsuspecting staff had not yet detected the cause of the restless behavior. Rusty and the chaplain stood near Reynaldo in quiet conversation.

"We appreciate these students who will share their talents with us. For the time they have spent rehearsing and for the staff who have encourage them. Now, let's get on with the show."

Dr. Lupenski walked off as the gold stage curtain opened slowly, after a couple of false starts, revealing a trio of musicians. They were still tuning their instruments—two guitars and a set of royal blue drums. Jock, the drummer, looked out of place with the other two who had long, wild hair. They wore torn jeans and vests, but no shirts. One sang and screamed the lyrics of a familiar heavy metal tune. The audience clapped and cheered.

The opening act was followed by Pete who ambled in front of the closed curtain, carrying his guitar and a wooden stool. Seated on the edge of the stool, he strummed and fingered a melody Rey recognized from Pete's rehearsal in the dorm. His long, sandy hair hid his face from view as he bent forward, watching his fingers at work. The audience became more restless and noisy. Rey was relieved when Pete ended his piece to a cacophony of hoots, impolite comments, and a token applause.

The fading noise resumed as the curtain opened again revealing a female form with hips swaying the provocative beat of taped music. "Go Francine," someone shouted from the back of the gym. As the tempo accelerated, the dance became more frenzied and suggestive. Francine, wearing a very short, tight black skirt and a low cut pink blouse, moved sensuously, encompassing the width and depth of the small stage. Some of the staff appeared in a state of panic, fearing a riot. A few of the noisy bunch were standing in their chairs, shouting encouragement to the gyrating dancer. Suddenly, the curtain began to close, and the music halted abruptly. The patients yelled in protest.

Rey overheard Rusty comment to several staff members, "Most of the patients are high on something. We've got to find out what and who's responsible."

As he spoke, Dr. Lupenski mounted the stage again. "The show is over," he announced loudly and sternly into the microphone. "Everyone go back to your dorms. Now!"

CHAPTER FOURTEEN

Laura Glover left the gym immediately. She was livid over the apparent drug infiltration and the revolting behavior of the patients. "Stupid kids," she muttered to herself as she walked rapidly toward the staff parking lot, beyond the fence. In her haste to return to the normalcy of her apartment, she ignored the standard procedure of never walking across the campus alone, after dark. Although the premises were generally well lit, there were a few shaded areas. It was as she rounded the corner of the education building that she became aware of someone following her. Her heart raced and her steps quickened toward the lighted area ahead. Suddenly, a strong arm pulled her backward as another arm circled her head, muffling a scream. The stalker wrestled her to the ground, clamping a hand over her mouth. My God, she thought, he's going to rape me. The shadowy figure was breathing heavily as his free hand groped at her clothing. The sound of running footsteps startled her attacker. He released her and broke into a run toward the fence.

"Mike," she whispered. "It's Mike."

"Are you alright?" Walt, the coach, extended his hands to help her up. She leaned on his wide chest and sobbed in relief. "Security will stop him. They've already been alerted. One of the staff saw him leave the group and start in this direction."

They watched as a security vehicle stopped just outside the fence and two security men ran toward Mike from opposite directions. For a moment, he looked like a trapped animal, uncertain which direction to run. Seeing no escape, he dropped to his knees and the two men each grabbed an arm and escorted him toward the parked vehicle.

"Let me walk you to your car," Walt said.

A chill shook Laura's petite frame. She accepted his offer, gratefully. The negative vibrations she had first received from Mike in her classroom had been an omen of this incident, she was convinced. As they neared the gate, they could see small clusters of patients being herded to the dorms. Many were still behaving erratically and shouting obscenities to no one in particular.

Often, Laura Glover had contemplated leaving the Pines for a "normal" teaching job, but she was convinced that these seemingly uncooperative, unyielding adolescents needed her special blend of firmness and compassion. Kids like Mike made her job particularly frustrating, but just frequently enough to feed her determination, a kid like Reynaldo Garcia would come along.

As if tuned into her thoughts, Walt asked, "Did you ever think of leaving this place? Finding a job in a regular high school?"

"Mm, hum, many times, but I like it here most of the time. I've had students in my class who made me nervous, but this is the first time I've ever been physically attacked."

They paused briefly while security personnel acknowledged them and opened the gate.

"How about you," she asked. "What keeps you here?"

"Same as you," he grinned. "Maybe, just maybe, I can make a difference in some of these kids' lives."

Laura stopped beside a white Toyota. "Well, here's my car. Thanks for saving me."

Walt squeezed her elbow and winked. "Any night of the week."

Laura turned the key in the ignition and looked back through the chain link fence where aides and security men were still trying to control groups of patients. The already hyper patients were angry because of the interruption of Francine's dance. Many had remained in the gym chanting "Francine, Francine," until the security guards were called. It was when they were told that security was "tied up" with another problem that word spread about Mike's attempted assault on Miss Glover.

"Security can't send anyone right now," Rusty reported to Dr. Lupenski. "Two men had to leave their posts to take Mike Thornberry to 'lock up'. He followed Miss Glover and attacked her." Lupenski's face turned as red as his beard.

"Tell Morrison to see me in the morning. We've got to 'beef up' security when we have these special events. No, never mind, I'm going to my office and call him now."

Finally, the available staff, mostly aides, was successful in steering the patients away from the gym. As Rey left, he noticed Chaplain Matherly talking to Francine.

Reynaldo had left the gym with Charles, but now he couldn't find him. The tall black boy's head was usually visible in any crowd, but he was nowhere in sight.

When they were finally inside the dorm, the hyper groups of boys were still complaining loudly and some were talking about Mike. Most were amused by his actions toward the young teacher. Reynaldo was not amused. He wished he could personally give Mike a punch in the stomach. Laura Glover was his friend. She had encouraged him and impressed on him the idea that he could learn and succeed. He hoped she wasn't hurt. Again, he looked around for Charles. Where was Charles?

"Where is Charles?" Rusty asked.

Reynaldo suddenly became worried, remembering Charles' concern about his mother after receiving the letter from home. Maybe he'd gone over the fence.

"Has anyone seen Charles?" Rusty asked again.

"He's probably down the highway, by now," Chino said through numb lips, his eyes dilated and wild looking.

Rusty went to the phone to call Security. "Go to your beds. Every one of you," Rusty ordered.

Reynaldo obeyed, gladly. He felt like an old man, tired and weary. He was angry at Charles for leaving. What did he think he could do for his family, anyway? He was still angry at Mike for his attack on Miss Glover— disgusted with Chino because of the drug incident, but still fearful of crossing him. He was hurt and disappointed because of Carmelita's apparent coolness toward him. Disappointed because he had not received one letter since his arrival. Jim Hagerty's search for relatives had turned up nothing. He wondered how long they would let him stay at the Pines. Where would he go if they let him out? He was determined not to "goof up: and risk being discharged early.

CHAPTER FIFTEEN

Most scheduled activities were cancelled the next day while the patients had extra counseling sessions with the caseworkers. The infiltration of drugs into the facility was of major concern and Dr. Lupenski was determined to get to the root of the matter. Every patient and staff member was subjected to drug screening—even off duty staff was called in.

"This is the second time during the past year that we had had an infiltration of drugs and I intend to stop it." Dr. Lupenski paced as he spoke to the assembled staff members. "If any of you have a clue concerning the source, I implore you to tell me. I will keep your name confidential. If one of you sitting here is guilty, I suggest you turn in your resignation immediately and save yourself some unpleasantness. A drug free environment is our first priority here, and we will not tolerate those who ignore that fact." He pounded a table top with his fist for emphasis.

Most of the group sat in stoic silence. A few whispered to each other. Juan Rivera glanced toward Larry McBride who leaned against the wall, with arms crossed over his chest. His expression was impassive. There was something about that guy that he didn't like, but he couldn't quite put his finger on it. Juan checked his watch and then bolted out the door. He was five minutes late for an appointment with Reynaldo. In spite of his determination not to do so, he was becoming very attached to this boy. During twelve years as a social worker, he had not dealt with a more appealing adolescent. Rey's small stature and baby face presented a disarming look of innocence.

Juan's experience had taught him, however, that all drug abusers were very manipulative and must be treated with caution. He was pleased that Reynaldo was "opening up" more and seemed more comfortable in their sessions.

He entered the office in a rush, just in time to catch a glimpse of Rey darting across the office and hastily taking a seat. He knew the boy had been up to something. Rey lowered his eyes as he tried to suppress a smile. Then, Juan noticed the room seemed strangely askew. The lemonade poster on the wall was upside down. His wife and kids were balanced on their heads, too. Everything in the room that could be moved easily was upside down—even the wastebasket. His first impulse was incredulity. Then, he realized the rearrangement was meant as a joke and began to laugh and shake his head.

"You little punk." He aimed a mock punch at Rey's shoulder.

Looking embarrassed, Rey attempted to smother his own laughter.

"Didn't you like my office like it was?"

Rey shrugged. "I don't know why I did it."

Juan thought he knew why. It was Rey's way of showing his feelings, not having the ability to put his feelings into words or to show overt affection. Conversely, Juan would have no problems expressing his affection for this young client, but must guard against being demonstrative. He must prepare Rey for a new life outside these fences and he knew Rey must not develop a psychological dependency on him or anyone else in the facility.

"Rey, I tried to contact your Aunt Maria at an address in Uvalde." He fingered a pencil on his desk and wished he could avoid seeing the disappointment in Rey's eyes.

Rey knew what was coming "She moved again, didn't she?" He tried to pretend that it didn't matter, but he found it hard to understand why she wouldn't at least write to him. In a few months, he would have to leave this place and go somewhere. But where?

Juan forced a smile and said with false optimism. "Jim Hagerty will find her." He still had not mentioned the possibility that Rey might have a grandmother still living. Hagerty hadn't located her yet, and it would be cruel to plant the seed of hope in Rey only to be disappointed again.

Juan stood and walked to the window, adjusting the blinds against the morning sun. "Rey, do you know anything about the cocaine that was smuggled inside the fence?"

Somehow Rey had not anticipated the question and it caught him off guard. His lips parted, but only a syllable escaped. He averted Juan's steady gaze, as he slowly shook his head. This was the second time he had lied in direct response to Juan's questioning, and he didn't like the way it made him feel. He remembered Chino's threats and wondered what would happen if he told the truth. He didn't wonder long because Juan dismissed him abruptly. "You can go now. Don't you have a ballgame this afternoon?"

Rey nodded and rushed for the door. As he left, he was aware of Juan turning the lemonade poster right side up. Juan was amused at Rey's prank but also confused by his response concerning the cocaine. His gut feeling was that Rey had information he was not disclosing. He also had a sneaking suspicion that his "bad boy", Chino had something to do with it. Maybe he would just have to confront Chino.

CHAPTER SIXTEEN

Jock sized up the batter at the plate, spit, and took his wind up. It was the seventh inning and the "Abusers" were behind by six runs. Jock's mind was apparently not on the game as he had just returned from a furlough visit home to see his father and new stepmother. The visit had not gone well. A solid hit sent a grounder to right field, and there were two men on base with no outs.

"Hi," Laura Glover greeted Juan and scooted over to make room for him on the weathered, wooden bench.

"It's warm out here for October," he said, removing his gray suede jacket. "I haven't seen you at the baseball field before."

"No, I've just taken a special interest in one of my students and wanted to watch him play ball." She didn't divulge the fact that she had also taken an interest in the good looking coach. "Isn't Reynaldo on your caseload?"

"Yes, he is." Juan didn't seem surprised that Reynaldo was the object of her interest. "Does he affect you like he does me?"

"Well, if you mean that you think he's adorable."

Juan seemed amused. "I wouldn't use that adjective, but he does . . . get to me."

Two more runs had widened the breach in the scores. Another crack of the bat sent the ball soaring past Reynaldo, who was at his usual post in left field. He had become overly cautious since his concussion.

"Hey, wake up, punk." Chino called from first base.

Rey shook his head in disgust and returned Chino's hateful stare. He scanned the small group of spectators for a glimpse of Carmelita. He hadn't seen her since the night of the talent show. He noticed the chaplain, in one of his brightly colored shirts, was third base umpire.

The opposing team from town had been dubbed "the straights" by their opponents, although their uniforms displayed "VFW Vets" in bold, black letters. The "Abusers" were not so uniform in appearance. They all wore gray sweat pants from the gym and assorted tee shirts.

"Looks like our boys are having a bad day," Juan said.

Laura nodded in agreement.

"Oh, Laura, I'm really sorry about the . . . the problem you had with Mike Thornberry after the talent show."

Laura muttered a soft "Thank you", and her eyes focused momentarily on a rock on the ground, which she pushed with her foot.

"Dr. Lupenski said he's already been discharged to his probation officer in Beaumont. He'll probably go to jail for a while."

"I'm relieved." Laura sighed and turned her attention to the game, with an occasional glance at the coach.

The game was now in the last inning and the Abusers were at bat. The fat boy hit a ground ball to infield and exerted much effort in running to the base, only to be thrown out. Next up was Rey, with Chino waiting in the "on deck" circle. A dark blue tee shirt hung loosely from Rey's narrow chest. He dug his heels into the dirt and choked up on the bat. Anger raged inside his short frame.

The bat connected with a slow pitched ball which popped high in center field. The excitement of the hit caused Rey to sling the bat recklessly, as he ran toward the base. Chino jumped aside and cursed the batter and the bat which almost hit his ankle. A tall, skinny guy caught the ball for the third out. The game was over.

The winners were shaking hands with the losers. "Good hit, buddy." The first baseman patted Rey on the back. Rey turned at the sound of Chino's angry voice. "Hey, you punk, you tried to hit me with that bat!" He grabbed a handful of Rey's shirt.

"It was an accident." Rey grabbed Chino's fist in both hands.

The confrontation was interrupted, as Juan approached. "Well, you guys lost, but no big deal. You played some good ball." Chino abruptly released his grip on Rey's shirt. Juan looked sternly at Chino and invited him to his office. "I think we need to have a talk, Chino."

Rey looked after the two figures as they left the field. He was worried. What if Juan had learned about Chino's role in Murphy's accident and the drug incident, and what if Chino thought . . . . His thoughts were interrupted by Owen Matherly.

"That was a good, solid hit, Rey." He flashed a friendly "thumbs up" gesture and placed a firm hand on Rey's shoulder. "Too bad it was caught. We might have had a rally right there at the end."

"Yeah," Rey said, not feeling like being drawn into conversation with the chaplain, especially since he had not attended chapel service as he had promised.

The winning team was loading their equipment into a van parked near the field. Rey noticed Walt and Laura Glover walking toward the gym together.

"I'd like to visit with you again Rey, but I know you need to get back to the dorm and I've got to go visit one of the girls who's discharging tomorrow. Come by my office when you have time." Matherly patted Rey's shoulder and started toward the girls' dorm.

Rey suddenly had an uneasy feeling in the pit of his stomach. "What girl is discharging?" He asked the retreating chaplain.

Owen Matherly did an about face, taking a couple of steps backwards as he acknowledged the question. "Carmelita Crain," he called back and then continued on his way.

The news hit where it hurt . . . deep inside; a feeling with which Rey was all too familiar. He stood alone and helpless in the middle of the empty field. His team members were all entering the gym to shower and change clothes, while Rey just stood there feeling as though the world was coming to an end. Some of the boys had commented that Carmelita was "knocked up", but he refused to believe it.

CHAPTER SEVENTEEN

After a fitfully sleepless night, Rey awoke to the protests of the others being awakened for the day's activities. Thoughts of Carmelita came rushing in, crowding out everything else. He knew she would be leaving and he would not see her again. Maybe if he "played sick", he would be sent over to detox. Since all patients entered and exited from that unit, there was a chance that he might at least see her.

"What's wrong with you this morning?" Auntie Bea made her second pass by his bed, genuine concern registered on her broad face.

Reynaldo faked a cough and placed a hand on his forehead. "I think I've got a fever."

Frowning, Auntie Bea replaced his hand with her own, "Yes, I believe you might have a little fever. I'll call detox and tell them you're coming over to a temp check."

The walk to detox was a short distance, past the canteen and cafeteria. A cool, brisk wind signaled the onset of fall. Reynaldo had been at the Pines for almost four months now and still no closer to locating his Aunt Maria. But, at the moment, he was more concerned about Carmelita and where she would be going.

A white station wagon, one belonging to the Pines car poor, waited near the front gates; a sure sign that someone was arriving or departing. His heart pounded fiercely beneath a faded black sweatshirt.

Rey pressed the buzzer on the door of the red brick building. A nurse he'd never seen before opened the door. "Are you Reynaldo Garcia?"

He nodded and stepped inside. His eager eyes surveyed the length of the long hallway, but no one was visible. Voices emerged from Dr. Benson's office where the door was partially opened.

"Go in the examination room and I'll be with you in just a minute." The nurse indicated the room where Reynaldo had first met Dr. Benson and Nurse Nancy. An involuntary shiver crept over him as he remembered the formidable nurse. For a moment he contemplated what might have happened to her after she left the Pines. Was she terrorizing patients somewhere else?

The voices from Dr. Benson's office spilled into the hallway and Rey was sure the feminine voice was Carmelita.

"Here is your ticket," Dr. Benson said. "You should be in Dallas by two this afternoon. Your mother will meet you, and here is the name of a doctor I want you to see. Take care of yourself."

"Thanks for everything, Dr. Benson."

The sound of her voice was irresistible and Rey stood framed in the doorway until their eyes met. She was holding one small bag and the security guard held another beat up black suitcase. For several poignant moments, there was neither sound nor motion.

"Goodbye, Rey," Carmelita said, softly, but her eyes spoke what her lips could not express. Rey could only stand in frozen silence as Dr. Benson accompanied her through the outside door.

Rey lay on his bed in the dorm, staring at the ceiling. His temperature was declared normal, but he had an excused absence from morning activities. He would miss a group therapy session, Miss Glover's class, and Auto Mechanics.

Auntie Bea stood by his bed again. "It's that girl, isn't it?" she asked kindly.

Rey looked surprised. How did she know about Carmelita?

As if reading his thoughts, she said, "I've seen you looking at her and talking to her over at the cafeteria. I heard yesterday that she was leaving."

A tear escaped from the corner of Rey's left eye. He was sure this was the first time he had shed tears since that awful bicycle accident when he was ten.

Auntie Bea patted his arm. "It'll be alright. You'll forget about her soon. That's the way it is with young love."

Rey didn't believe her, but he was grateful for her concern. Again, that overwhelming feeling of familiarity descended upon him. Who did this woman remind him of? She certainly didn't resemble his mother or his Aunt Maria.

By noon, Rey was up and on his way to the cafeteria for lunch, although he didn't feel hungry. Soon, he was at a table with Pete and Jock, listlessly playing with a plate of spaghetti. Behind them was the usual group of Hispanics—Chino's friends. Ever since Murphy's unfortunate "accident" in the restroom, Rey had tried to avoid this group as much as possible. Chino was missing from the group. They seemed agitated and chattered in loud whispers, speaking in both Spanish and English. Rey overheard bits and pieces that sounded like, "Chino nearly killed and something about a car falling and Murphy's name.

"You missed all the excitement, man," Jock was saying. "Murphy tried to get Chino . . . a car was on the hydraulic lift . . . Chino was underneath . . . Murphy had left the car in neutral . . . it rolled off and if Chino hadn't moved like lightening, he'd have been crushed." Jock spoke with an overloaded fork suspended between his plate and mouth.

Then Pete took over. Rey had not heard more than two words out of him before and didn't know he stuttered. "Th-then M-Murphy and Ch-Chino got into a r-real f-fight."

Jock took over again, with his mouth still half full of spaghetti. "Chino threw a tire tool at Murphy and barely missed his head. Then Murphy grabbed a can of Freon and sprayed Chino before Mr. Mason could break it up. Two security guys came and took them both to isolation."

Rey felt disappointed that he had not been present to witness the scene. He'd been hoping that Murphy could somehow "repay" Chino. If he were not so fearful of Chino, he'd like to have a shot at him, himself.

After lunch, Pete accompanied Rey to the gym where they were scheduled for weight training and conditioning. Regular use of the weight equipment was creating bulges in Rey's forearms, shoulders, and thighs. He had even grown three-fourths of an inch taller since being at the Pines. He was now a strapping five feet and five and one quarter inches tall.

The combination gym and auditorium also housed an indoor swimming pool where a small group of people were gathered near one end. They were not in swimsuits. Rey eyed them with curiosity.

"W-w-wonder w-what's g-going on? Pete said.

They stood some distance apart until Rey recognized Owen Matherly in the group. Standing beside him was Francine. Both wore shorts and tank tops. Rey moved closer as the two descended the four steps into the shallow end of the pool.

"Francine is getting baptized," a girl Rey didn't know by name volunteered.

Baptized? Rey didn't know big people were baptized. He knew that he had been baptized as a baby. Aunt Maria told him so. He watched, fascinated, as the chaplain raised one hand and said, "In the name of the father, the son, and the holy ghost," before plunging Francine beneath the water for a brief moment. She arose, brushing the long, wet strands of blonde hair from her face.

Her caseworker and the no-name girl accompanied Francine as she left the pool, wrapped in a large white towel. Owen Matherly knotted a similar towel around his hips and approached Rey and Pete.

"Hey, Rey, did you ever witness a baptism before?" Not waiting for an answer, he continued. "Come to the chapel Sunday and you'll see a different Francine. She's going to sing at the service . . . you too, Pete." He walked on past, but turned back. "Oh, Rey. Carmelita left something for you. I'll give it to you Sunday morning at the service." Then, he turned abruptly and left the gym.

Carmelita left something? He was tempted to run after the chaplain and ask what it was, but he decided he'd have to wait. Sunday would be the day after tomorrow. That seemed like a long time to wait and wonder.

CHAPTER EIGHTEEN

Actually, there was no chapel at the Pines. "Chapel" services were held each Sunday morning in the recreation hall by the indescribable Owen Matherly. Attendance was optional, and most patients opted to go back to the day rooms after breakfast, to watch old movies or hard rock videos or just to rehash old squabbles with each other and the staff.

On this particular cool November morning, however, Rey was the first one there, eager to see what Carmelita had left him. The chaplain was rearranging the chairs when Rey entered quietly, and waited to be noticed.

"Rey, come on over here and give me a hand. I need some help moving this table."

Rey complied. As they set the table against a wall, Matherly said, "I think I know why you're here this morning. Am I right?"

He forced eye contact with Rey and coaxed a smile from him. "I've tried to get you to chapel for months now, but it took a present from a girl to finally get you here," he teased.

Reaching inside the pocket of a jacket draped over the back of a chair, he pulled out a small box. Before Rey could open the box, Francine appeared, carrying a guitar. While she and the chaplain discussed when she would sing, and where, Rey settled into one of the metal folding chairs, next to the wall. He noticed a quickening of his heartbeat, an occurrence reserved for unusual events, as he anticipated the contents of the tiny box. Lifting the lid carefully, he found a crumpled silver chain, with a silver heart dangling from it. Several others had arrived for the morning service.

To avoid the eyes of the curious, Rey returned the chain to its box without further inspection. The fact that she left something for him made him feel very special. It proved she really liked him.

Rey tried to concentrate on the words that Mr. Matherly was expressing with great conviction. He was able to grasp fragments of sentences such as "drugs create problems" . . . "you were created in the image of God." Rey's hand kept slipping into his pocket, fingering the silver chain. His thoughts kept drifting toward Carmelita, and memories of her long, dark hair, flashing eyes and pink lips. Once, when his mind returned to the speaker, he heard the chaplain saying, "You are all here because you have problems . . . some you could have helped, some you could not. But, you can still overcome those problems and make something beautiful of your life. Trust in God to help you." Suddenly, Rey thought of the lemonade poster in Juan's office and thought he understood its meaning; then there was a flicker of understanding, and then an involuntary smile.

The chaplain finished his remarks and concluded with a short prayer. He uttered "Amen" and called Francine to sing. She sat on the edge of the table against the wall, balancing a guitar on her lap. A full, black and white skirt draped her crossed legs and touched her ankles. She wore a white turtleneck sweater. Her long hair was pulled back in a ponytail and tied with a black ribbon. There was definitely something different about Francine. Was it her makeup? She still had it on. Was it the hairdo? Reynaldo had seen her with her hair pulled back before. No, it was something in her expression; something in her eyes. She strummed the guitar and sang in a clear voice . . . a song about a "woman at the well". Rey was puzzled by this new Francine. She hardly seemed like the same girl whose erotic dance had created such a sensation only a few weeks ago.

After the service, Rey did not hang around to talk to the chaplain, again because several others had gathered around him and Francine. He and Pete went on back to the dorm, since it was still an hour until lunch. A white station wagon parked at the front gate drew his attention. At some one hundred yards distance, he couldn't be sure, but the tall black boy emerging from the station wagon looked very much like Charles. Could it be? He stopped in his tracks and stared until the boy and driver disappeared inside the detox unit.

"That looked like Charles," he muttered to himself as much as to Pete who had stopped alongside him.

He had heard nothing about his friend since the night he went over the fence, after the talent show. Once, in the hall outside Juan's office, he had passed Charles' caseworker, Cathy. He had an impulse to stop her and ask about Charles, but he didn't. He had missed Charles' broad smile and good humor, and though he wished him no bad luck, he would be glad to see him again. Since his absence, and then, Carmelita's departure, Rey had felt lonely and restless. Now, he didn't even have baseball to sustain him. The baseball equipment was traded for basketball and Walter was having them practice dribbling and shooting baskets. Rey didn't like basketball as he was too short for the sport.

There was not much activity in the dorm. Some of the boys were still lying on their beds or sitting in groups, probably plotting their mischief of the day. With few scheduled activities on the weekends, the residents became easily restless and bored.

"How are you feeling today, Rey?" Did you get over your fever?" Auntie Bea asked in mock seriousness.

Rey knew that she knew he hadn't been sick; not unless being heartsick can be called an illness. Suddenly he remembered the necklace in his pocket, and giving Auntie Bea one of his rare smiles, he went on to his bed and in semi-privacy, discovered the dangling heart would open. Forcing a fingernail inside the seam, he carefully opened it and there was Carmelita staring back at him from a tiny photograph. Her expression seemed almost apologetic. He would treasure this keepsake always, but he knew with certainty that he would never see her again.

A week later, Charles was back in the dorm. The reappearance of the black boy made Rey realize how much he had missed his friend's cheerfulness and good humor. It seemed as if the cloud that descended since Carmelita's departure, had now vanished.

"Hey, little buddy, tell me what's been happenin'? Did you miss me?" That wide, toothy grin lit up Charles' face. The two of them were sitting at one of the card tables. Rey absently shuffled a deck of cards. Charles had been released from detox that day. He was held there for a week, not because he had drugs in his system, but because he had a slight case of the flu.

"Do you have to go through the whole program again?" Rey asked. "You already had six months."

"Hey, man, you know I love this place. I had my vacation, but I had to come back and see about my little buddy."

"How's your mother?" Rey asked, wondering if he would get any straight answers from this joker.

Suddenly, he looked quite serious. "She's better. She's home now. My sister, Marcelle, is out on parole, and she's staying with her. Someone got Marcelle a job at an electronics company. With that and the welfare payments, maybe they can get by." Charles picked up the cards and started dealing with his long fingers. Rey had always been fascinated by the length of Charles' fingers.

"What happened to that chick you had the 'hots' for? Carmelita; is she still here?"

"No. she was discharged." Rey looked out the window at the deepening shadows. It seemed that darkness came earlier every day. He considered showing the locket to Charles, but decided not to. The locket would just remain his private possession; his only link with Carmelita.

Sensing that Rey didn't want to talk about Carmelita, Charles quickly moved on to someone else. "I heard Francine got religion. Glory, hallelujah!" He said with mock fervor. "The devil's loss is the Lord's gain." He shook his head, grinning, remembering Francine's dance at the talent show.

"I went to chapel last Sunday," Rey volunteered.

Charles slapped the corner of the table and laid down his cards. "Well, glory hallelujah again, little buddy. What's this world comin' to?"

"Francine sang a song and played a guitar. She seemed . . . different."

They were silent for a few moments, each looking over their cards. Several other guys were watching a movie on TV and ignoring them completely.

"Charles, did you see Chino over there in detox?"

Charles looked up. "Yeah, he's supposed to get out tomorrow. I mean, back over here. Murphy is being discharged as soon as his probation officer can send someone to pick him up." He laid his cards on the table. "There's a new aide on the evening shift that told me all that stuff."

"Where's McBride?" Rey asked, with sharpened interest.

"He was fired; didn't you know?"

A frown appeared across Rey's forehead, as he slowly shook his head.

"They found out he was dealin' man. Dr. Benson called the DA, and he'll probably go to jail." Charles emitted a wicked laugh. "Now, I'm really worried; who's going to bring me my drugs?" He laughed again. "Your bid, little buddy."

Charles won every game. Rey could not concentrate for worrying about McBride's firing and what Chino might be thinking.

"When are you getting out, little buddy? You've been here since last May. You gonna grow old in here with me?" Charles smoothly captured Reynaldo's hand by playing three aces.

Rey shifted in his chair and looked out the window at the darkness beyond. "I don't know. I'm supposed to see Juan tomorrow and talk about it." He quietly accepted the next hand Charles dealt, thinking about the world outside the chain link fence. Where would he go? What would he do? What would that world be like for him?

CHAPTER NINETEEN

A cool, fine mist fell as Rey hurried to keep his appointment with Juan. He didn't know why he hurried, because Juan was usually late. Not because he was derelict of his duties; just the opposite. He often consulted with others on the staff concerning his clients. As Rey suspected, no one was in the office when he arrived. A private smile emerged as Rey recalled his childish prank of last week. He had been sort of embarrassed after he'd done it and hadn't told anyone. He really wished he hadn't been so impulsive. Juan probably considered his actions a sign of immaturity, and one thing Rey didn't want to be called was "immature".

He sat down and immediately noticed a file folder in the center of Juan's desk with his name on the label. GARCIA, REYNALDO—ADMITTED 05-12-89 C.O.P. He had learned that meant condition of probation. A desire to peek inside the folder overwhelmed him. He went to the door to see if Juan was anywhere near. All he saw were secretaries concentrating on their work. He quickly went to the desk and opened the folder without picking it up. His picture and some vital statistics about him were inside the front cover. On the other side a letter caught his attention. He recognized Jim Hagerty's signature. He glanced toward the open door again as he started to read.

Dear Mr. Rivera:

Pursuant to your telephone request of November 21, 1989, I am writing to inform you of my conversation with Mr. and Mrs. Albert Gonzales, former foster parents of

Reynaldo Garcia. They have informed me that it will not
be possible to take Reynaldo back into their home. They
are fearful that he might be a negative influence on their
three children . . .

Rey heard Juan's voice as he spoke to the secretary just outside the
door, and frantically scurried for a chair. He didn't want to be caught again
in some deed of misbehavior. The news contained in the letter stunned
him. Giving up on ever hearing from his Aunt, he had built his hopes on
returning to the Gonzales home. They were a real nice couple with three
young children. Tears had started gathering in his eyes even before Juan
got to his desk. Simultaneously, each of them noticed the open file on the
desk.

Juan looked at Rey disapprovingly. Noticing the beginning of tears,
Juan picked up the letter. "Did you finish the letter, Rey?"

Feeling defeated, Rey just shook his head. He didn't know that another
letter in the file reported on Jim Hagerty's conversation with Reynaldo's
grandmother. She hadn't made a commitment yet to take Rey and it
wouldn't be fair to mention her just yet.

"I know you are disappointed about the Gonzales family, but don't
worry, we won't put you out until suitable living arrangements are made.
Since you will soon be 16, we might be able to get you into the Job
Corps."

Rey had heard about the Job Corp from Pete. Pete had been in the Job
Corps and run away. That was why he was at the Pines. Previously, Pete
had been in a private drug treatment program, in South Texas. Pete said
the Job Corps worked twelve hours a day and "the supervisor was always
on our backs". The Job Corps didn't sound like a very good alternative to
Rey, but, what else could he do? He wished he could just stay inside these
fences. His bed was comfortable; he was eating three times a day. Several
people were very kind to him . . . Juan, Auntie Bea, Miss Glover, Dr. Benson,
Walt, and Chaplain Matherly. He felt very safe here, except for Chino. The
remembrance of Chino caused him to shudder.

"Are you cold?" Juan asked. "It's getting colder outside, but after all,
it's almost Christmas. I noticed some Christmas decorations going up this
morning."

The mention of Christmas plunged Rey into a deeper state of despair. Not that his Christmases had been so great, but last Christmas he'd been with the Gonzales family, and they had treated him as one of the family, giving him gifts and eagerly sharing all the festivities. The memory pained him, especially because of what he'd done after—joining his friends on a drinking spree and being an accomplice to robbery. He didn't blame the family for not wanting him back.

"I see your birthday is right after Christmas . . . the 28th." Juan was still thumbing through the file.

Rey's mood took another dip. Birthdays were especially difficult. For years, Rey hadn't even known they were an occasion to be observed. Then, one year he and Maria's daughter, Yolanda, were invited to a neighbor's party. It was the first time he'd seen a birthday cake with candles and it made a big impression. The boy's mother had baked it and seemed to enjoy the party as much as the children.

His thoughts were interrupted again by the sound of Juan's voice. "Rey, Miss Glover says that you are now doing some ninth grade work in English. That's good." Juan spoke with his usual enthusiasm. Reynaldo half-listened to his "pep" talk, while entertaining feelings of anger and depression which had been building for some time; it's not fair, he thought. It's not my fault my mother died, and my dad left. It's not really my fault that I'm here now, and have no place to go.

As he stood up to leave Juan's office, the lemonade poster caught his eye. "Humph," he muttered to himself, "I don't even like lemonade."

CHAPTER TWENTY

Jim Hagerty leaned back in his swivel chair, his booted feet adding to the clutter on his desk. A Styrofoam cup of coffee was growing cold as he leafed through the Reynaldo Garcia file for the third time since arriving at the office. He had misplaced the grandmother's phone number. She hadn't returned his call and it had been two months since they talked. It was becoming urgent that he make some arrangements for the kid. They wouldn't keep him forever at the Pines.

What was that doctor's name? Barton? Benjamin? Something that started with a "B". A copy of a letter he had mailed to Maria Vasquez the previous month stopped his search momentarily. Ah, the boy's aunt. He wondered if he would hear from her again. The Vasquez family had been very elusive the past year. He had received one phone call from the aunt who was in Louisiana at the time. She didn't give him an address, because they were about to move again. Then, about six weeks ago, he had received a letter from Brownsville. Well, he thought, at least the aunt is interested. So many of the kids on his caseload had no one who really cared about them. The courts were backlogged with juvenile cases, and what was to be done with all of them?

He reached for his smoldering cigarette and overturned his coffee. "Damn," he muttered, dragging his feet from the desk and opening the bottom drawer where he kept a roll of paper towels. This had happened before. While cleaning the drips off the floor, a small piece of paper caught his eye; on it was the name Dr. Aaron Bergman, El Paso, and a phone number. He breathed a sigh of relief and checked his watch. It was almost noon; maybe he should just wait until after lunch to make the call. Mrs. Garcia was probably busy cooking. He reached for his Stetson and almost reached the door when the phone stopped him. "Damn," he said, already beginning to taste that bowl of hot, peppery chili at Fernando's diner. He grabbed for the phone, overturning the full ashtray.

"Damn," he repeated his favorite cuss word before pushing the extension button. "Hagerty here . . . Yeah, Rivera, what's up?"

Juan Rivera was deep in thought after his conversation with Hagerty. Dr. Lupenski was beginning to put some pressure on him to find a place for Reynaldo.

"He's not a bad kid," Lupenski had said only last week. "I think a longer stay in here will do him no good. He needs some time on the outside, and he hasn't even had a furlough."

"There's been no place to send him," his frustrated caseworker replied. Rivera had patiently explained that there were no relatives available to take him and the couple who had been his foster parents so briefly, refused to take him back.

The possibility that he might return to his aunt seemed out of the question. Rivera could only hope that the grandmother might take him for a couple of years. Then, perhaps he could make it on his own. Mason at auto mechanics said Rey was developing into a fair mechanic.

Rivera checked his watch. There was one more phone call he had to make today-to Dallas County probation offices, regarding one Thomas Delgado. "Chino" had been through the Pines drug treatment program twice without making any apparent improvement. When he was confronted with this fact and questioned about the incident with Murphy, he became very defensive.

"I'm doing as good as anyone in this place," he said. "I get up on time, I go to the cafeteria. I don't cut in line. I eat the same slop everybody else eats, and I don't complain about it." His upturned chin and half closed eyes indicated the attitude he adopted when challenging someone.

Rivera had dealt with many teenage boys who were very much like this one. They were alternately defensive or aggressive, and always defiant. He recognized that much of the tough exteriors they presented could be attributed to situations that began in early childhood. The vast majority had no father figures and mothers too busy trying to make ends meet to have time for them. Many had alcoholic and abusive parents; trying to reverse the effects of their upbringing was extremely difficult and many times impossible. In Chino's situation, he felt the latter was true. There was nothing more he could do for this client.

Chino had refused to admit any knowledge of Murphy's accident or the drug infiltration.

"Did someone tell you I was involved in these things?" he asked, warily.

Rivera had dismissed Chino following their conversation with a warning to "watch your step", knowing that keeping him at the Pines would only result in other incidents.

He dialed the Dallas County probation offices.

"Doyle Willis please. This is Juan Rivera." Hearing that Willis was out for lunch, Juan looked at his watch.

"Just tell him to return my call. I need to talk about Thomas Delgado."

CHAPTER TWENTY-ONE

Rey hurried from the auto mechanics shop to the A&E building. A cold December wind whistled through the tall pine trees beyond the fence. It penetrated his thin nylon jacket and tossed his coarse black hair about. Miss Glover asked him to stop by the library on his way to her class and select a novel to read. "The Last of the Mohicans" was the first book he had ever finished and he liked it. Since then, he had read several books from beginning to end.

Knowing the librarian always complained about dirty hands on "her" books, Rey stopped at the restroom to wash up. He was just drying his hands with a paper towel when the door opened and Chino appeared.

"Hi, Chino. How're you doin'?" He tried to appear "cool", although a cold fear gripped him.

Chino looked toward the door and then in one swift motion grabbed Rey's shirt and pinned him against the wall. "Not so good. Someone squealed on McBride and I figure it was you . . . you little punk." A fist hit Rey squarely on his left jaw and sent him to the floor.

The jaw ached and his elbow that hit the floor was in pain, but Rey felt a sudden surge of courage. If he could get off the floor, he felt he could damage this long haired bad guy. "Where are your helpers?" Rey asked with bravado, as he tried to get up. Before he could get to his feet, however, Chino came at him again. Taking a calculated risk, he stayed on the floor and raised both feet, kicking at Chino as hard as he could, and sent him crashing into the lavatory behind him.

Attracted by the noise, Owen Matherly appeared at the door. He looked surprised to find Reynaldo there. As Chino made a move toward the chaplain, Dr. Griffin looked in, also attracted by the noise. He quickly assessed the situation.

"I'll go call security," Griffin said as he disappeared.

Chino pushed past the chaplain and went out the door. Rey was now on his feet and trying to decide which part of his body hurt more, his jaw or the elbow.

The chaplain started inspecting Reynaldo to see how badly he was hurt. "We better get you over to Dr. Benson and let him look at this jaw." The two of them walked into the hallway and saw no one. The altercation occurred in the same restroom where Chino and his friends had attacked Murphy.

"Security probably has Chino in hand by now," Matherly said. "Is your leg hurt?" Reynaldo limped slightly although he had not been aware of hurting his leg. Before they exited the building, Juan met them in the hall.

"What happened?" He asked. His brow wrinkled in concern.

Owen Matherly volunteered all the information he knew, as they continued their slow walk. Juan walked out the door with them. All three stopped, all eyes focused on the fence about sixty yards in front of them.

Chino balanced precariously atop the inside chain link fence which was about twelve feet high. Two security guards on the ground were shouting at him to come down. Chino shouted back curses and obscenities.

"Owen, you walk Rey on over to see Dr. Benson. I'll go out and try to talk Chino down."

As Rey and the chaplain continued their walk toward detox, Rey looked over his shoulder as Juan neared the fence. He wished they would just let Chino keep going. This place would be much better off without him.

One of the familiar white station wagons waited near the entrance to detox, with the motor running. "Jock is being discharged," the chaplain said. "He's going to live with his mother in Abilene."

Just before entering the detox building, Rey looked back toward the fence again and saw that Chino was down, alongside Juan and the security guards. They appeared to be in heated conversation.

As was his custom, Dr. Benson was giving Jock some last minute advice before his departure. Jock had been behind these fences less time that Rey. At least he had a home to go to.

Rey and Matherly waited in the treatment room for Dr. Benson to appear. Rey was remembering the day he waited here alone when Carmelita was preparing to leave.

"I had a letter from Francine," the chaplain was saying. She had been discharged the week before. "Her probation officer helped her get a job in a supermarket. She's also helping part time at a Crisis Center."

Rey was reminded that only he and Charles still remained of those who were in detox back in May. Juan and Dr. Benson appeared in the treatment room at the same time. Rey was aware of a throbbing pain in his elbow. The jaw hurt a little less.

"What happened to you?" Dr. Benson asked.

"One bad boy named Chino roughed him up a bit," Juan volunteered, "but he won't be doing any more damage around here. He's in seclusion and will stay there until the Dallas County Sheriff Department comes for him, probably tomorrow."

The doctor inspected the swollen jaw and gently moved Rey's arm.

"Ouch," Rey winced.

"We better X-ray that arm."

The chaplain excused himself, but Juan remained until the X-ray had been done. While the two awaited the verdict from Dr. Benson, Juan planted a hand on Rey's shoulder and looked him square in the eyes.

"Rey, I have good news, but so much has been happening, I didn't have a chance to tell you. Are you ready?"

Rey's pulse quickened. He took a quick breath and waited expectantly. Juan had heard from his Aunt Maria.

"Rey, Jim Hagerty located your grandmother in El Paso. Your father's mother, Florencia Garcia. She took care of you when your mother died. She wants you to come live with her." He spoke the words slowly and evenly, his eyes never leaving Rey's. He knew it would be difficult for Rey to assimilate this startling revelation. The boy could not respond. He was speechless.

Dr. Benson returned, holding an X-ray which he clipped to a viewer on the wall and flipped on a light. "There's a hairline fracture just below the elbow. We'll have to splint the arm for about six weeks. The jaw will just have to heal on its own, and it will, just like the knot on your forehead did.

Only then, did the doctor turn to look at Rey, who still sat there dumbfounded. He couldn't speak. This day had been too eventful for words.

CHAPTER TWENTY-TWO

It felt weird having a cast on his arm. A bright blue sling held the arm taut against Rey's chest. Although he was right handed, he'd never thought about the handicap of being able to use only one arm. Charles had helped him get dressed each morning since the "accident", two weeks ago. Now, the tall black boy was helping him put his few belongings into the same duffle bag he'd carried into the facility almost seven months ago. In some ways, it seemed he'd been inside these fences all his life and a few of these people were as close to being "family" as anyone he'd known.

"How far is it to El Paso?" Rey asked his friend.

"I've never been there, but its way down there, almost in Mexico. You'll be on that bus nearly all night."

An unspoken sadness had settled over the two boys. Rey was thrilled and excited about living with his grandmother, but he would miss Charles' broad grin and good humor.

Rey had talked to his grandmother on the phone from Juan's office, two days after Chino departed. He had cried tears of happiness at hearing the voice of his very own grandmother. He had also talked to her employer, Dr. Bergman, who made it clear what he expected.

"You can work on the grounds a couple of hours each day to pay for your room and board. I understand you're a pretty good mechanic. You can help take care of my car and pickup, too. You behave yourself, and we'll get along just fine."

Rey tried to conjure up images of Dr. Bergman and his grandmother. He wondered what they would look like. Somehow he knew his grandmother would be plump, with a broad, pleasant face. Suddenly he was struck with the realization that . . . that . . . Auntie Bea . . . yes, Auntie Bea reminded him of his grandmother.

"What's wrong, little buddy?" Charles asked, noticing Rey's far-off stare.

Reynaldo had stopped midway of trying to separate his personal items from those belonging to others. He stared out the window at the cold misty rain that fell intermittently.

"Oh, nothing. Just wondering if it's raining in El Paso too."

"Naw, it's probably sunshine and 80 degrees."

The last items Rey removed from the drawer by his bed were a small Bible given to him by the chaplain and the small box in which he received Carmelita's locket. The silver chain and heart, with Carmelita's photo was concealed beneath his black sweatshirt. Someday he hoped to go to Dallas and find her.

"If I ever find my way to El Paso, I'll look you up, little buddy. If you're going to school, you should try to play baseball. You've got some talent," Charles grinned. "You never know about me. I might end up playing basketball with the Los Angeles Lakers." He faked a jump shot into an imaginary basket.

Rey was aware that Charles' caseworker was trying to get him a college scholarship.

"In three weeks, I'll be finished with my Algebra II and English III; then I'll be on my way, man. Onward and upward." Charles snapped his fingers and executed a couple of "jive" steps. They both laughed, dispelling the mood that had persisted since the first news of Rey's impending departure.

Rey left the duffle bag while he ran to the A&E building, to see Miss Glover. She had asked him to come by before he left. As he entered the classroom, Walt was just leaving. Rey had seen the two together frequently the last couple of months.

"Good luck," the coach said, shaking Rey's right hand. "Keep playing ball. You'll make some coach a great outfielder."

Rising from her desk, Miss Glover smiled sweetly. "Rey, I'm going to miss you. You are one of the best students I've had. Next fall you'll be ready to start your sophomore year in high school and that's good." The teacher hugged him clumsily, trying to avoid contact with his injured arm. "Take this book with you," she said. "Maybe you can read it on the bus."

Rey accepted the book and read the title, "The Red Badge of Courage". He wanted to say something. He wanted to tell her how much he liked her and how good he felt about being able to learn from her teaching, but there was something in his throat, and he just couldn't speak. He managed a sort of smile and turned abruptly and left. He hoped she understood.

Before leaving the building, he went hurriedly toward the chaplain's office. Juan had told him to be at detox by 10 a.m. He would meet him there, but Rey just had to say goodbye to Owen Matherly. The only route to the chaplain's office was past the infamous restroom. The confrontations that occurred there were still very prominent in his mind, but, in time, he hoped the memories would fade. He wanted to put all that behind him.

The chaplain's office was empty. Rey stood still for a full half-minute, his eyes saying a silent goodbye to the books, the plaques, and picture on the walls, and the open Bible on the desk. All these things seemed important to Owen Matherly, and Rey did not want to forget him.

A white station wagon waited near the entrance to the detox unit. Rey handed his duffle bag to the security guard nearby. Inside the building, Juan and Dr. Benson were waiting for him. Dr. Benson gave his cast, sling, and arm a final check-up. Rey supposed this would be his last visit to this room. He reviewed his previous visits here . . . that evening which now seemed long ago, when he first arrived . . . Nurse Nancy . . . the day he was knocked unconscious by the baseball . . . waiting here to catch a final glimpse of Carmelita.

"In a couple of weeks you need to get your grandmother to take you to a doctor in El Paso to check on this," Dr. Benson was saying. "Here's a few Tylenol you can take if the arm gets too uncomfortable on the bus ride."

He handed him a small plastic container with five or six white tablets inside.

"Here's your bus ticket," Juan said, handing him an envelope with his name printed on it. "You will have an hour lay-over in Dallas. Just stay in the bus terminal and you shouldn't have any trouble." Juan's hand rested on Rey's shoulder as they moved toward the door. "Jim Hagerty will call you at your grandmother's. You will still be on probation for a few more months."

Dr. Benson opened the door and the three of them stepped out into the emerging sunlight. The dark, threatening clouds were beginning to break up and move on. A security guard sat in the driver's seat waiting, the motor idling.

"After you get settled down in El Paso, let me hear from you. I want to know how you're doing."

Another lump invaded Rey's throat. He recalled the strangeness of the place upon his arrival and how isolated and formidable it all seemed. Now, it felt like "home", and he was heading for new surroundings.

As he was about to climb into the waiting car, he heard his name from a distance. It was the chaplain, who was jogging toward them. He was almost breathless when he reached the car.

"Rey . . . good luck, Rey; God Bless You," he said, patting him gently on the back.

"Goodbye," Rey managed a smile.

As the car door closed behind him, his eyes lingered on the faces of Dr. Benson, Juan, and the chaplain.

Owen Matherly beamed a smile, and signaled his now familiar "thumbs up" symbol.

As the gates swung open and the car backed out slowly, a tall black boy in the distance waved "goodbye" to his little buddy.